Breaking
The Chains

Books by William Loren Katz

EYEWITNESS: THE NEGRO IN AMERICAN HISTORY

TEACHERS' GUIDE TO AMERICAN NEGRO HISTORY

FIVE SLAVE NARRATIVES

AMERICAN MAJORITIES AND MINORITIES: A SYLLABUS OF U.S. HISTORY FOR SECONDARY SCHOOLS

THE BLACK WEST: A PICTORIAL HISTORY

THE CONSTITUTIONAL AMENDMENTS

A HISTORY OF BLACK AMERICANS

THE CIVIL WAR: A GUIDE TO BLACK STUDIES RESOURCES

RECONSTRUCTION: A GUIDE TO BLACK STUDIES RESOURCES

MINORITIES IN AMERICAN HISTORY, SIX VOLUMES

MAKING OUR WAY: AMERICA AT THE TURN OF THE CENTURY IN THE WORDS OF THE POOR AND THE POWERLESS

BLACK PEOPLE WHO MADE THE OLD WEST

THE GREAT DEPRESSION

NAZISM

THE INVISIBLE EMPIRE: THE KU KLUX KLAN IMPACT ON HISTORY

Published by Atheneum

BLACK INDIANS: A HIDDEN HERITAGE

THE LINCOLN BRIGADE (WITH MARC CRAWFORD)

BREAKING THE CHAINS: AFRICAN-AMERICAN SLAVE RESISTANCE

BREAKING
THE CHAINS

African-American Slave Resistance

William Loren Katz

Atheneum   New York

Collier Macmillan Canada
Toronto

Maxwell Macmillan International Publishing Group
New York   Oxford   Singapore   Sydney

...sistance, and To Laurie

Atheneum
Macmillan Publishing Company
866 Third Avenue, New York, NY 10022

Collier Macmillan Canada, Inc.
1200 Eglinton Avenue East
Suite 200
Don Mills, Ontario M3C 3N1

Printed in the United States of America
Designed by Nancy B. Williams
10 9 8 7 6 5 4

Library of Congress Cataloging-in-Publication Data
Katz, William Loren.
Breaking the chains: African-American slave resistance/by William Loren Katz;
illustrated with prints and photographs.
—1st ed.   p.   cm.
Includes bibliographical references.
Summary: Describes slavery in the United States, the harsh conditions under
which slaves lived, the active and passive resistance with which they fought for their
rights, the revolts, and the involvement of slaves in the Civil War.
ISBN 0–689–31493–0
1. Slavery—United States—Insurrections, etc.—Juvenile literature. 2. Southern
States—History—1775–1865—Juvenile literature. 3. United States—History—Civil War,
1861–1865—Afro-Americans—Juvenile literature. 4. United States—History—Civil
War, 1861–1865—Participation, Afro-American—Juvenile literature. [1. Slavery. 2.
Slavery—Insurrections, etc. 3. United States—History—Civil War,
1861–1865—Afro-Americans.] I. Title.
E447.K38 1990 975'.00496073—dc20
89–36355 CIP AC

The author wishes to thank Dr. John Henrik Clarke, professor emeritus, Department of Africana and Puerto Rican Studies, Hunter College, for his careful review of the manuscript.

Table of Contents

Introduction

Heroic men and women crowd the pages of U.S. history and punctuate its major events—defiant minutemen at Concord Bridge; brave pioneers plunging into the wilderness; intrepid Marines at Wake Island refusing to surrender; daring astronauts.

Africans who arrived here on slave ships have not been part of this glorious heritage. When American courage is celebrated, slaves are left out. The story of their heroism has not often been told because history was recorded by those who sold, owned, or profited from their labor.

To justify their profits from bondage, masters invented useful tales. They insisted Africans were an inferior breed who benefited from the culture of their European and Christian owners. Vice President John C. Calhoun, a famous South Carolina master, said bondage made Africans "so civilized and so improved, not only physically, but morally and intellectually." To excuse kidnapping Africans from their families and homeland, Virginia planter George Fitzhugh insisted slaves "love their master and his family and the attachment is reciprocated."

Fitzhugh and Calhoun claimed Africans in slavery not only enjoyed hard work in the hot sun but were happier than any other laborers in the world. To justify enslavement, masters bent history, truth, and the Bible to their purposes. They also created their own "scientific evidence." Dr. Samuel Cartwright of the University of Louisiana said blacks "consume less oxygen than the white" and this fact "thus makes it a mercy and a blessing to negroes to have persons in authority set over them, to provide and take care of them."

Central to the slaveholders' reasoning was the lie that Africans willingly accepted slavery and rejected rebellion. Dr. Cartwright claimed "there had never been an insurrection" against slaveholder rule. When slaves tried to escape, the doctor called it "Draptomania, or the Disease Causing Negroes to Run Away." When blacks rebelled, sabotaged production, and fought white masters and overseers, it was "Dysthesia Aethiopica," a mental disorder "peculiar to Africans."

The lies of slaveholders did not die quickly or easily. In 1863, after thousands of blacks had fled plantations to fight for liberty in the Civil War, Confederate president Jefferson Davis still called slaves "peaceful and contented laborers." The Civil War ended slavery, but scholars and textbook writers carried on the planters' view of the happy, dull, docile slave. An ex-Confederate soldier, John W. Burgess, became a noted historian at Columbia University. He influenced generations of scholars with his views that African Americans were inferior to whites and content under slavery.

Thus, the slave owners' version of slave life had a lasting impact on historians from the North and South. Scholar William E. Woodward wrote that African Americans were the only people in history emancipated "without any effort of their own," and two of this country's most liberal and famous historians, Allan Nevins and Henry Steele Commager, wrote college texts that emphasized slaves were attached to their masters, "well cared for and apparently happy."

The story of Dred Scott illustrates the way slaves were presented as pathetic stereotypes. Because of the Supreme Court case that bears his name, Scott has always been the one black figure in U.S. history courses. But little is said about him as a person— that he saw his first wife and two children sold away, that he married Harriet, and they had two children, Eliza and Lizzie, whom he desperately wanted to live in freedom.

Historians wrote about a Dred Scott who was "lazy and shiftless." Some even ridiculed him as a carefree, stupid man with no real interest in freedom. In *American Heritage*, famous Civil War historian Bruce Catton said Scott was "a man without energy" and attributed to Scott such words as his "case was 'a heap o trouble,' " and "he was amazed at all 'de fuss day made dar in Washington.' "

In fact, Scott shouldered huge burdens to lift slavery from his family. For a time he escaped to the Lucas Swamps outside St. Louis, a haven for slave runaways. Then he was recaptured and brought back. After that he mainly spent time working at extra jobs, raising cash to purchase his family's liberty. When his owner, Mrs. Emerson, turned down the $300 he had saved, Scott hired a lawyer and brought his case before Judge Krum in St. Louis.

Despite rapidly deteriorating health and the onset of old age, Scott pursued this legal effort for ten years and ten months. Along the way he received some financial help from antislavery whites.

Though the Supreme Court ruled against the Scotts, a new master soon freed them. The Scotts worked in St. Louis, Dred as a porter at Barnum's Hotel and Harriet running a laundry business, with Dred helping her out after hours.

The real Scott story turns out to be one of courage and endurance by a family committed to liberty. But they never really had their day in court because they faced an all-white Supreme Court stacked against them. Then later scholars emphasized this distorted, stereotyped image.

Such fantasies about slaves reached generations of teachers, textbook authors, and Hollywood writers. Their words and images penetrated millions of young U.S. minds.

The seventh and eighth graders who entered my New York City classroom in the 1950s knew their slavery lessons cold. "Slaves didn't really mind it," said one, "because it wasn't so bad." "If they didn't like it, they would've revolted," said another. "Slavery was really like a kind of social security," said a third. No one seemed to disagree with these views that they had been taught in elementary school.

To those reared on this version, it seemed un-American to depict the evils of slavery and disloyal to talk about African-American people fighting for freedom against whites. Omitting, neglecting, or suppressing the facts of slave defiance became a lasting American tradition.

The truth about bondage was always available. Before the Emancipation Proclamation, slave men and women escaped and wrote more than a hundred autobiographies and published seventeen newspapers. Antislavery or abolitionist publications of the nineteenth century bulge with black and white testimony exposing the evils of bondage. Six thousand pages of the recollections of ex-slaves are on file at the Library of Congress, and hundreds of other interviews are kept at Fisk University. Most scholars have ignored this mountain of evidence. Some flatly said that while those who profited from slavery could be objective, those who suffered from it lacked powers of observation or sufficient detachment to judge fairly.

Slave testimony reveals a heritage of rebelliousness stretching from the kidnappings in Africa to the end of the Civil War, and this American story adds a proud new dimension to the world struggle for freedom. Africans demonstrated endurance, resilience, and bravery in the face of the most wretched conditions in the New World. They were among the first Americans to die for the great ideal that all are created free and equal.

Today the story of slave resistance can be described with a high degree of accuracy through accounts left by the men, women, and children held in bondage and their relatives and friends. I have chosen to construct this book largely based on their testimony, and I have also included the recollections of white slaveholders and their families, foreign visitors, military and government reports, newspapers, and legal records.

Because this book is short and focuses on the black contribution to emancipation, white participation, since it appears in many other books, is indicated but not fully examined. It was the resistance of the slaves that, each step of the way, galvanized whites and free blacks into action.

All quotations are by blacks, slave or free, unless otherwise identified. Some African-American narrators, such as Frederick Douglass and Harriet Tubman, have recently found their place in school courses. But other witnesses are largely unknown. Some left scant identification in the historical record except a few words, and a first or last name. Others left even less—a nickname, a state, a date. In telling their stories, some did not wish to give their name. More often the man or woman who took down their words did not bother to ask for one. I have included whatever information is known of these people whose surviving words bear witness to our common history.

William Loren Katz

Fighting Bondage on Land and Sea

The First Rebels

ONE

Slavery in the New World began the day Christopher Columbus landed. "I took some of the natives by force," the explorer wrote in his diary on October 12, 1492. In 1498, British explorer John Cabot seized three Native Americans. By 1524, when Giovanni da Verrazano arrived, he found Native Americans who "are suspicious, hostile, and desirous of obtaining steel implements for defense against kidnappers, who frequent the coast to seize and transport them to the Spanish Islands of the West Indies."

From Canada to Florida, forced Indian labor became a thriving European business in North America. Colonizing powers seized Indians and battled each other for domination of a continent. In the next century and a half, international wars engulfed the Americas. When Native American nations along the Atlantic coast were attacked by white settlers, their males were killed, and their widows and orphans were rounded up for sale or exchange.

The French in the Ohio valley, Louisiana territory, and Canada became active traders. In 1684, King Louis XIV of France announced "these savages are strong and robust" and ordered that Iroquois captives be made to serve on French vessels. In Canada, French officials enslaved Pawnees, and along the Mississippi valley they kidnapped the Natchez.

In British America, the trade in Indians shaped colonial diplomatic, political, and economic policies. The money made by British slavers helped colonial commerce and filled colonial treasuries. Captive Indians became forced apprentices in Connecticut. They were given as pay and as bonuses to soldiers in Virginia and Massachusetts. In Rhode Island, Maryland, North Carolina, and South Carolina, they became the leading source of colonial revenue.

The trade in Indian slaves, at first run by speculators, soon spread to governors, businessmen, and aristocrats. In 1712, North Carolina's Governor Hyde expressed his pleasure with "the great advantage that may be made of slaves, there being many hundreds of them, women and children." Three years later, South Carolina missionary the Reverend M. Johnson said "our military men were . . . so desirous to enrich themselves by taking all the Indians slaves."

Enslaving natives was not without severe problems. Relatives of the captured counterattacked or offered refuge to runaways. Indians were able to escape to the forests and hills they knew better than their masters. Relatives of those kidnapped living in heavily armed neighboring nations gave British frontier families nervous and sleepless nights. The colonists, convinced that this slave-taking threatened their lives, began to seek changes. Some demanded this slavery stop; others insisted that local Indian captives be sold or shipped far from their homeland.

Finally, colonial legislatures passed laws for "transportation" of seized Indians to distant lands. This would be the first but not the last time that resistance to the slave system would alter the rules governing the business.

Long before they seized Africans, Europeans had learned it is best to keep slaves far from their homes and natural allies. Indians taken in New England were sent to the West Indies; those seized in the South were traded in the Caribbean, New England, or the Middle Colonies. In 1707, the governor and Council of South Carolina listed "Boston, Rhode Island, Pennsylvania, New York, and Virginia" among "places we export Indian slaves."

Indian slavery began to decline. Native people died of disease and overwork. Nations retreated into the wilderness to fight. Condemnation of Indian slavery in the Spanish colonies by Bishop Bartolomé Las Casas in 1514, and his suggestion of African labor, led traders increasingly to a new source. By the late 1600s, the vast majority of American slaves were Africans.

A people brought three thousand miles from home had no one to turn to. Without others in the Americas who looked like them, Africans who fled their chains could easily be tracked and recaptured. No escape, no friends, and no hope, reasoned Europeans, would soon make frightened, discouraged Africans accept their lot. Traders felt they had found a unique solution.

The first Africans were led aboard ships that celebrated Christianity—*Gift of God, Jesus, Mary.* They were packed into vessels named for admired friends—*Elizabeth, Robert, William, Judith, Little George, Young Hero, Don Carlos.* They sailed on ships that celebrated great virtues—*Justice, Hope, Liberty, Fortune, Charity, Integrity, Friendship, Good Intent.* Divided from others of their nation, shackled hand and foot to people who did not speak their language, they spent seven to eight weeks on the stormy Atlantic.

Kings, queens, merchants, nobles, and bankers made huge profits from the voyages. But the hard and heartless work was carried out by smiling or mean-spirited captains and underpaid, mistreated crews. Some officers tried to keep the Africans healthy and alive to make the most money from them. Others packed Africans into every corner of their tiny ships. Though many

Under watchful eyes, Africans are loaded aboard ships to the Americas.

would die this way, they calculated, the many survivors would still insure profits.

Gustavus Vasa described his confinement: "The closeness of the place, and the heat of the climate, added to the number in the ship, which was so crowded that each had scarcely room to turn himself, almost suffocated us."

Dr. Falconbridge, a ship's surgeon, reported to Parliament how he "wedged them in. They had not so much room as a man in his coffin either in length or breadth." But when Dr. Falconbridge crawled among the chained men, they "bit and pinched him."

It was commonly said of slave ships, "You could smell them five miles downwind."

Some pious officers brought Africans on deck each day for Christian worship services or the singing of psalms. Captain John

Hawkins's sailing orders were: "Serve God daily, love one another, preserve your victuals, beware of fire, and keep good company."

In 1562, Hawkins launched the English slave trade with a few small ships, one hundred crewmen and three hundred captured African men, women, and children. Queen Elizabeth first denounced his effort and said it was "detestable and would call down vengeance from heaven." But after she saw Captain Hawkins's huge profit, she became a major shareholder in his next African expedition.

The right to supply Spain's American colonies with slaves was a prize eagerly sought by businessmen from Holland, France, Denmark, England, Prussia, Spain, and Portugal. In 1713, the English gained it by treaty. A British scholar reported that the slave trade "became the daily bread of the most considerable part of British manufacturers." Money from this trade helped finance the British industrial revolution and built the ports of Bristol and Liverpool. "There was not a brick in the city but was cemented with the blood of a slave," said a Bristol resident.

Slave traders became welcome guests in churches, palaces, and parliaments. In 1757, a British slave merchant returned home after eleven years to find he had many friends, was welcomed "at every great man's house," and was called The African Gentleman. He heard his adventures on the high seas compared to Columbus's expedition.

European traders carried off Africa's strongest sons and daughters. With bribes and guns they convinced the chiefs of African villages to sell their prisoners and to organize manhunting expeditions. Europeans skillfully played on local rivalries in an Africa as divided as Europe was.

The foreigners promised to pay handsomely for the captives. Europeans exploited disputes among African nations and fostered rivalries between kings. Soon African nations were pitted against one another in wars to turn neighbors into slaves.

About a third of the men, women, and children captured in the slave wars died on the long trip that brought them from Africa's interior to the foreign ships at the coast. Others died while the ships swayed at anchor off the coast, and still others died in the long voyage across the Atlantic.

The captives once had lived and worked in happy families. They were diamond, gold, and iron miners, weavers or potters. Many from along the coast or lakes fished for a living. Some worked in bronze, copper, or gold or traded with Asians, Europeans, and other Africans. Some were farmers or herders and others were musicians, priests, and royalty. But now, kings and commoners were packed into narrow holds of foreign ships.

While their homeland was still in sight, men and women took every opportunity to rebel. "We shackle the men two and two, while we lie in port, and in sight of their own country, for 'tis then they attempt to make their escape and mutiny," reported a captain in 1693. "We always keep sentinels upon the hatchways, and have a chest full of small arms, ready loaded, constantly lying at hand, together with some grenade shells, and two of our quarterdeck guns pointing on the deck, and two more out of steerage."

There were many desperate efforts to rebel and return home while the ships were in sight of the African coast. A Dutch slave ship anchored in Africa's Gulf of Guinea around 1699 had to battle African captives who "unknown to any of the ship's crew, possessed themselves of a hammer [and] broke all their fetters in pieces." The Africans "came above deck and fell upon our men." Their victory was interrupted when a French ship and a British ship arrived. The combined foreign force killed twenty and drove the Africans belowdecks.

In 1734, Samuel Waldo, owner of the *Africa*, commanded his captain and crew to place many armed guards and "put not too

Slave revolts rocked the African slave trade. This is a French drawing.

much confidence in the Women and Children lest they happen to be instrumental to your being surprised which might be fatal."

In 1757, natives from shore attacked several slave vessels in the harbor and liberated their friends and relatives. Two years later on the Gambia River when eighty Africans rebelled, a wounded captain fired his gun into the ammunition room and the ship exploded.

A crewman aboard a New England ship anchored off the African coast reported: "The Negroes got to the powder and Arms at about 3 in the morning, rose upon the whites, and after wounding all of them . . . ran the vessel ashore . . . and made their escape."

Slavers knew they carried the most dangerous cargo in the world. In 1776, Edward Long characterized Africans as "wolves or wild boars" who committed "many acts of violence . . . murdering whole crews, destroying ships when they had it in their power to do so." Captives were carefully guarded, and heavily armed crewmen stood ready to crush rebellions. Captains brutally enforced Captain William Snelgrave's advice in 1727 that "no one that killed a white Man should be spared."

Sometimes captives found or made weapons. Aboard the British vessel *Don Carlos,* Africans made knives, "pieces of iron they had torn off our forecastle floor," and struck at a crew already weak from disease. Guns saved the whites, reported one. "We stood in arms, firing on the revolted slaves of whom we killed some, and wounded many, which so terrified the rest that they gave way."

To keep prisoners weak, desperate, and quiet, food and water were cut. To reduce resistance through terror, captains ordered public executions at sea, and torture of any who appeared rebellious. The resistance did not end.

To keep them in good physical condition after so many hours in chains belowdecks, Africans were brought on deck each day for what Dr. Thomas Trotter called "dancing the slaves." With guns trained on them, they were prodded to dance and sing.

Captives gave voice to familiar music to express their deep longing for home and establish a bond among the many tongues. A British doctor on the *Young Hero* wrote: "They sing, but not for their amusement. The captain ordered them to sing, and they sang songs of sorrow. Their sickness, fear of being beaten, their hunger, and the memory of their country . . . are the usual subjects."

Another doctor at night heard "howling melancholy noise, expressive of extreme anguish." An African woman explained her people had awakened after dreaming of their own country to find themselves in a slave ship. The men and women cried, "*Kicheraboo,*" which meant, "We are dying."

Whether they were watched carefully or casually, treated badly or well, Africans wanted most to return home to freedom. In 1727, one British captain thought a more charitable and friendly

Africans aboard slavers. If they could not revolt, they tried to throw themselves overboard or starve themselves to death. At right, a man is forced to eat.

approach might win cooperation from his human cargo. For nine days he joined Africans at mealtime, sitting on deck, eating with them out of the small bowls. On the tenth day, reported a crewman, they "beat out his Brains with the little tubs."

Europeans mistakenly assumed that their captives had no knowledge of navigation and once at sea would have to accept their fate. But some 150 recorded rebellions at sea marked the centuries of the slave trade. In 1701, there was a shipboard revolt in which twenty-eight Africans were killed or "leapt overboard, and drowned themselves in the ocean with much resolution, showing no manner of concern for life," reported a white crewman.

In 1730, about ninety-six Africans aboard the *Little George* slipped out of their chains and overpowered the crew. When some armed crewmen hid in a cabin, they were left alone, their door guarded. The black rebels concentrated on sailing back to Africa, which they accomplished in nine days.

Two years later Africans slew the captain of the *William*, set the crew adrift, and also returned home.

Women, allowed more freedom on deck and at night, were at times able to play a key role in mutinies at sea. In 1721, a woman aboard the *Robert* off the coast of Sierra Leone served as a spy for a "Captain Tomba," who led a revolt. She sounded the signal, and with Tomba and another man, killed two of the crew. Tomba, the unknown woman, and the mutineers were overwhelmed by crewmen with muskets.

Captain Philip Drake, a slaver for fifty years, said: "Slavery is a dangerous business at sea as well as ashore." But the transatlantic trade, fueled by its staggering profits, continued despite its rebellions and despite the "rights of man" promised by the American and French revolutions. It was not outlawed by nations until the early nineteenth century.

Africans arrived in the New World weary, undernourished, and sometimes racked with disease. Many had suffered disabling injuries and some were near death. Recalled Charles Ball: "More than a third of us died on the passage, and when we arrived in Charleston, I was not able to stand. It was more than a week after I left the ship before I could straighten my limbs."

Most Africans were not sent to North America directly. They were put through a "seasoning" process in the West Indies, which taught them the language, religion, and demands of their captors. A third died resisting the process of seasoning.

Only a year after the first Africans walked down the gangplank in Hispaniola in the West Indies in 1502, Governor Nicolas de Ovando reported they were fleeing to Native Americans and could not be recaptured. King Ferdinand of Spain, convinced of terrible danger, ended the slave trade. But economic considerations soon overrode fear, and the business reopened.

Slave rebellions erupted on the Caribbean island of Hispaniola in 1522, in South Carolina in 1526, in Puerto Rico in 1527 and 1533, in Panama in 1531, Mexico City, 1537, Havana, 1538, Honduras, 1548. After the Mexican revolt, the slave trade was again banned by Spain for eight years.

In 1542, an archdeacon informed authorities in Hispaniola that "no slave is reliable" and "they have more freedom than we have." Four years later a report claimed seven thousand had liberated themselves "each with spears they had stolen from fallen Spaniards." "No one dared to venture out unless he was in a group of 15 or 20 people," it said. "We lived in constant fear," admitted a Spaniard.

Europeans tried to end resistance. Dogs were trained to hunt runaways. Rebels or escapees were branded or tortured. A death penalty hung over anyone who aided runaways or rebels.

Thousands of fugitives, or maroons as they were called, survived in strongly defended colonies located in distant, remote regions. Their armies challenged the foreign invaders, and their farmers and traders competed with Spain's. In 1545, maroons in Hispaniola turned down Spain's offer of peace, saying they could not trust Spaniards. The next year a Spanish court announced that maroons had become so potent a force that planters only dared issue gentle orders to slaves.

During the seventeenth century, the Republic of Palmares, a maroon settlement of ten thousand in northeastern Brazil, prospered. Its soldiers drove back a dozen Dutch and Portuguese armies sent to demolish it "by fire and sword."

In Palmares and in the slave huts of the Americas, black and red people met and married. This biracial history is captured in the sacred legends of the Saramaka people (dating from 1685) of Dutch Guiana, now Suriname. The African leader of the Saramakas, Lánu, was a slave who ran to the woods after his wife was

Throughout the Americas, slaves—African and Indian—fled, armed, and formed outlaw colonies in the wilderness. French historians called these maroon colonies "the gangrene of colonial society."

slain. According to Saramaka legend, Wámba, the forest spirit, appeared: "And Wámba came into Lánu's head, and brought him directly to where some Indians lived. These Indians welcomed him, and gave him food. And he lived with them there."

When Lanu's younger brother Ayakô fled slavery, Lánu "found him and saw that he had been well taken care of by the Indians, that he had done well there. He, too, found many things to eat there." Native American aid for Lánu and Ayakô symbolizes a rebirth of Saramaka people beyond the eyes of their foes. It also describes a common alliance forged by Africans and Indians.

Captain John Stedman spent years as a mercenary for the Dutch in the Guianas. His deadly enemies were the maroon descendants of Lánu and Ayakô. In 1776, he wrote: "The Negroes are spirited and brave, patient in adversity, meeting death and torture with most undaunted fortitude, their conduct in the most trying situations approaching even to heroism."

Daily Toil, Perilous Struggle

A Troublesome Property

T W O

The reason for slave resistance was slavery. Masters, whether
kind or mean, quickly learned that bondage bred defiance. In
1794, President George Washington wrote that he expected slaves
"to be a very troublesome species of property."

In 1750, a quarter of a million people in British America were
enslaved, and by the time of the Declaration of Independence the
number had doubled. Slavery gradually disappeared in the North
after the Revolution. But it remained a part of life in the South,
and by 1860, fourteen states held 4 million Africans in chains.

Frederick Douglass escaped slavery at twenty-one. His written
and spoken words perceptively analyzed the system's evils. In one
speech he described the condition of bondage: "The law gives the
master absolute power over the slave. He may work him, flog
him, hire him out, sell him, and in certain instances, kill him, with
perfect immunity. The slave is a human being divested of all
rights—reduced to the level of a brute—a mere 'chattel' in the eye
of the law—placed beyond the circle of human brotherhood—cut
off from his kind—his name . . . inserted in a master's ledger, with

In 1860, Thomas Drayton of Hilton Head, South Carolina, armed more than one hundred slaves. Some are shown in this photograph after their liberation by the U.S. Army-Navy.

horses, sheep, and swine. In law, the slave has no wife, no children, no country, and no home. He can own nothing, possess nothing, acquire nothing."

In 1860, 350,000 white families held slaves, and many other southern whites had an economic stake in bondage, or thought they did. African Americans raised 90 percent of all cotton, an even larger percentage of Virginia's tobacco, and almost all of Kentucky's hemp, Louisiana's sugar, and Carolina's rice. Slave crops provided the South's wealth, were its leading exports, and insured its economic growth. Slave ownership was the largest single economic interest in the United States.

The owners of slaves, especially the richest three thousand, dominated southern life. "The slaveholders are the South," wrote Douglass. "They are the only active power there. They rule the states entirely and tolerate no policy which in the least degree endangers their power." He said that the eight million whites who owned no one were "freight cars attached to a slaveholder locomotive. Where the locomotives go, the train must follow."

In the North, tax money built libraries and public schools. In the South, it built jails to hold slaves and paid the salaries of slave patrols. New York State published more newspapers than the fourteen slave states combined. "There is no legislation except for the benefit of slavery and slaveholders" in the South, wrote Hinton Helper. A nonslaveholder in North Carolina, Helper blamed the South's economic and educational problems on slavery.

At first, some slaveholders were tormented over their ownership of human property. Patriot Patrick Henry said: "Every thinking honest man rejects slavery in Speculation, how few in practice? Would anyone believe that I am Master of slaves of my own purchase? I am drawn along by the general inconvenience of living without them; I will not, I cannot justify it."

Then the invention of the cotton gin in 1793 made slavery a high-profit business. By quickly cleaning cotton of its seeds, the gin reduced the price of cotton. Slaves who once spent days picking out cotton seeds by hand were sent into the fields. The price of cotton fell and demand for it increased. Profits soared.

Planters who originally justified slavery as "economically necessary" now happily called it "a positive good." They claimed it was beneficial to white and black. Some began to argue that slaves were better treated than free workers and that perhaps slavery would be a good way to handle lower-class white labor.

Slave conditions varied widely from one plantation or master to another, but generally they were harsh. In the drive to maximize profits, owners showed little concern for human health and

safety. The cost of feeding a field hand on a plantation of a
hundred or more was about $7.50 a year. In the Georgia Sea
Islands standard plantation allotments were a peck of corn, a
pound of salt pork or beef every week or two, vegetables in
season, a little salt, and molasses. Clothing was a crude cloth outfit
issued in the spring and another in the fall. Shoes were handed
out once a year, a blanket every three years. Boys and girls
younger than thirteen were not given clothing. Slave families
lived in crude huts.

Contempt for life was built into a system whose goal was to
secure the largest profit possible from a people who had no rights.
In 1809, a South Carolina court ruled that "young slaves . . . stand
on the same footing as other animals." In 1844, Senator John
Hammond wrote of two of his workers who had died: "Neither

Slavery reduced human beings to chattel or
property, as in this notice of a raffle.

a serious loss. One valuable mule also died." Slaves were sold at auction, won in lotteries, lost at cards, or handed out as presents at birthdays, weddings, and Christmas parties.

Masters came to believe their race was born to rule, and their slaves were an inferior breed. Racial contempt led to cruelty. A Louisiana woman said: "I was once whipped because I said to missus, 'My mother sent me.' We were not allowed to call our mammies 'mother.' It made it come too near the way of the white folks."

Roberta Manson recalled: "They said we had no souls, that we were animals." She remembered her father was whipped "because he looked at a slave they killed, and cried." In 1854, a British official visiting South Carolina reported: "It is literally no more to kill a slave than to shoot a dog."

To insure a smooth working system, whites set about convincing Africans to obey their every command. Control of slaves' minds rested on denying them all knowledge of the world and constantly stressing that they were born inferior. "We knowed jess what they told us and no more," remembered William Johnson. Whites considered stupidity among slaves "a high virtue," said a slave who fled to freedom. Slave Edward Taylor recalled: "I thought white folks made the stars, sun, and everything on earth. I knowed nothing but to be driven and beat all the time."

The entire system was based on distortions and lies about race. Trusted slaves helped run plantations, kept records, and created useful inventions—but Africans were called an inferior breed. British journalist William Howard Russell found contradictions on a Louisiana sugar plantation. "The first place I visited with the overseer was a new sugar-house, which negro carpenters and masons were engaged in erecting. It would have been amusing, had not the subject been so grave, to hear the overseer's praises of the intelligence and skill of these workmen, and his boast that they did all the work of skilled labourers on the estate, and then listen to him, in a few minutes . . . on the utter helplessness and ignorance of the black race, their incapacity to do any good, or even to take care of themselves."

Planters liked to believe that African Americans, even those who carried out important responsibilities, were dependent on whites. Slaves without masters, planters thought, could not work for themselves. They would die without white managers. Ignored were the achievements of thousands of former slaves—even in the South—who became inventors, poets, teachers, ministers, or businesspeople. A plantation mistress who insisted her slaves "cannot take care of themselves," admitted they did everything. "I never so much as washed out a pocket handkerchief with my own hands," she remembered. Planters were dependent on slave labor for their wealth and leisure.

Visitors to the South, such as Harriet Martineau, reported insensitivity to pain, "savage violence," a rigidity of mind, and a "blunted moral sense . . . among the best whites." *New York Times* reporter Frederick Olmsted found little regard in many southerners for "the sacredness of human life." A black child received her worst whipping for playing with a doll that belonged to her owner's family. A hungry child was beaten for eating a biscuit.

Slavery as a form of violence encouraged more disorder. "Every natural and social feeling and affection are violated with indifference; slaves are treated as though they did not possess them," wrote Sarah Grimke, daughter of an aristocratic South Carolina family. She and her sister Angelina left the South to become noted antislavery writers and lecturers in the North. The Grimke sisters found "the system of espionage . . . over slaves the most intolerable known."

Planters made all the rules and faced no intervention from government or moral outrage from church. They could drive slaves as long as they wished. Edgar Fripp had his "work all night by the light of the full moon during some heavy periods." Women worked as hard as men, one recalling, "I had to do everything dey was to do on de outside. Work in de field, chop

Men and women shared the burdens of slavery.

wood, hoe corn. . . . I have done everything on a farm what a man done 'cept cut wheat. I splits rails like a man, I drive the gin, what was run by two mules." On one plantation, workers complained they hardly had time to eat, "hardly time to get a little water."

On large plantations owners handed control to overseers who acted as managers. Reporter Olmsted was told by an Alabamian that "a real devil of an overseer would get almost any wages he'd ask" and "if they made plenty of cotton, the owners never asked how many niggers they killed." When Olmsted asked if slaves weren't too valuable to abuse or kill, he was told, "Seems they don't think so. They are always bragging—you must have heard them—how many bales their overseer has made. . . . They never think of anything else."

Slave marriages were dependent upon the owner's permission. Since masters did not accept black marriages as binding, they refused to grant dignified weddings. They did not permit a minister or an exchange of vows; the loving couple was simply asked to jump over a broomstick.

Masters liked to think of themselves as kindly ladies and gentlemen converting childlike, ignorant heathens into civilized, Christian workers. "We never thought of them as slaves; they were 'ours,' our own dear black folks," said a Florida woman.

"They joyed with us and sorrowed with us; they wept when we wept, and laughed when we laughed. Often our best friends, they were rarely our worst enemies," recalled a Richmond woman.

Slaves had little choice but to follow their owners' demands and to live with their insulting attitudes. Once out of master's reach, however, slaves showed they had not been fooled. Jarmain Loguen fled bondage, wrote a book, became a noted New York minister and leading abolitionist voice. One day his old mistress wrote and angrily asked him for $1,000 for running away. She argued, "We raised you as we did our own children." The Reverend Mr. Loguen replied, "Woman, did you raise your own children for the market? Did you raise them for the whipping post? . . . Shame on you."

Despite planters' efforts at mind control, African Americans were guided by their own sense of dignity, morality, and community. William Craft's old master had a reputation of being a devout Christian, "but he thought nothing of selling my poor old father, and dear aged mother, at separate times, to different persons, to be dragged off never to behold each other again," wrote Craft. He "also sold a dear brother and sister, in the same manner as he did my father and mother. The reason . . . 'they were getting old, and would soon become valueless in the market.' "

For the African-American community the breakup of families through sale or auction was one of the worst threats of slave life. Josiah Henson was about six when an auction divided his family. His mother, older brothers, and sisters were sold first. "Then I was offered to the assembled purchasers. My mother, half distracted with the thought of parting forever from all her children, pushed through the crowd, while the bidding for me was going on, to the spot where Riley [her owner] was standing. She fell at his feet and clung to his knees, entreating him in tones that a mother can only command, to buy her baby as well as herself, and spare to her one, at least, of her little ones." Riley kicked and struck at her until she had to crawl away.

Once he escaped, Henson wrote a book of his experiences, helped other slaves escape, and became the model that novelist Harriet Beecher Stowe used for her lead character in *Uncle Tom's Cabin.*

"Slaves are taught ignorance as we teach our children knowledge," recalled Leonard Black. They were not told their ages, and those near water were not allowed to learn to swim. They were told free states were ten thousand miles away, and that whites who called themselves abolitionists would eat them.

James W. C. Pennington received a doctorate degree from Heidelberg University in Germany, and in 1841 he wrote the first textbook history of African Americans. But as a slave until he was twenty-one, "I was as profoundly ignorant as a child of five years old."

Finding that intelligence, knowledge, and talents might arouse

Above: During an auction, a slave mother is inspected by a bidder.

Below: Notice of a sale in 1852.

GANG OF 25 SEA ISLAND
COTTON AND RICE NEGROES,
By LOUIS D. DE SAUSSURE.

On *THURSDAY* the 25th Sept., 1852, at 11 o'clock, A.M., will be sold at RYAN'S MART, in Chalmers Street, in the City of Charleston,

A prime gang of 25 Negroes, accustomed to the culture of Sea Island Cotton and Rice.

CONDITIONS. — One-half Cash, balance by Bond, bearing interest from day of sale, payable in one and two years, to be secured by a mortgage of the negroes and approved personal security. • Purchasers to pay for papers.

suspicion or jealousy, slaves often played dumb. Lunsford Lane ran a profitable tobacco business, owned property, saved money, and "I never appeared to be so intelligent as I was." Blacks pretended to be meek, happy, and dumb. They learned to answer a master's questions with the words he wanted to hear. To fool whites, recalled Betty Jones of Virginia, people said, "Going to see Jenny tonight," which meant there was going to be a dance.

Henry Bibb concluded that "the only weapon of self-defense I could use successfully was that of deception." African Americans developed deception to a high art. "Got one mind for the boss to see, got another for what I know is me," went a slave song. A worker who laughed with his master in the afternoon might plan to escape that evening.

Laborers became too ignorant to do a decent day's work and too dense to understand or remember orders. "Under the cloak of great stupidity," said a Virginia planter, slaves made "dupes" of whites. Masters and overseers did not know when their hands were ill or just shamming, really physically disabled or just putting on a limp, a bent back, blindness, pregnancy.

In the evening among loved ones, souls were soothed with humor and faith to try to restore hope. People dreamed of, sang songs about, and prayed to God for deliverance. Solomon Northup, captured as a free man living in the North and held in bondage for twelve years, played his violin softly at midnight. "Had it not been for my beloved violin, I scarcely can conceive how I could have endured the long years of bondage." His autobiography tells the story of his kidnapping and his final escape.

Around quiet campfires or in the privacy of their huts, the slave community gathered to swap tales of turtles that outdistanced hares, of little Davids who slew huge Goliaths, and of tiny animals that tricked lions and bears who wanted to eat them. People nourished morale with jokes about refusing to be buried near their masters because the devil might take the wrong body.

Delia, a North Carolina cook, secretly expressed her rage in the kitchen. "How many times I spit in the biscuits and peed in the coffee just to get back at them mean white folks."

Slaves saw "good Christians" abusing their families and friends. Married white planters and their teenage sons slipped down to the slave quarter at night to find young women. The African-American community expressed its shock at "the devilment in the big house" and at such hypocritical Christians.

The oppressed noted where the arms were stored, when patrols rode by, and when masters and overseers went to sleep. The news was passed along to everyone in the community who could be trusted, and it mysteriously traveled through dense woods, over high mountains, and across wide rivers. Vice President John Adams was told by two French travelers who had visited the South, "The negroes have a wonderful art of communicating intelligence among themselves. It will run several hundred miles in a week or fortnight."

"Our police regulations are very defective," complained one slaveholder. Plantation security was not defective. It was being tested at all hours by people whose aim in life was to be free.

Plantation owners, judges, and legislators often missed this point. A 1669 Virginia law referred to "the obstinacy" of Africans. In 1758, a Florida slaveholder was shocked to learn his slaves were part of a conspiracy to achieve freedom. He wrote: "Of what avail is kindness . . . when rewarded by such ingratitude." In 1802, a South Carolina judge called African Americans "in general a headstrong, stubborn race of people." And in 1859, a South Carolina committee complained of their "insolence . . . as a race."

A people whose heritage was independence never surrendered its desire to return to its homeland or restore its original rights. Its women had special reasons for wanting to throw off their burdensome chains and return with their families to a life built on freedom.

The Battle for Family and Knowledge

THREE

Protecting family unity became the African-American community's first line of defense. A strong, united family provided the love, hope, and courage necessary for survival in a hostile land. In fighting for family, each individual knew he or she was not alone and affirmed a vital sense of identity and self-worth. The family unit's strength became the psychological base from which other resistance was launched.

Women and men labored together in the fields and shared the burdens and joys of home and family. Because of this, the division of labor between men and women that was so pronounced among Europeans never hardened in slave communities.

Powerful bonds of family love and kinship originated in West Africa, and slaveholders early sought to destroy African-American ties to the ancestral homeland. First banned was the use of drums, the center of African communications, and use of African languages. Whites also stopped non-Christian religious practices and cultural festivals.

The oppressor promoted his religion and culture to help install slave obedience and conformity. But in the privacy of huts, Afri-

Four generations of a slave family were still united as free people in Beaufort, South Carolina.

can traditions and words survived in secret. African respect for the elderly and care for children continued in New World communities. In the homeland, babies were named for dead or elderly kinfolk. Grandparents or elderly uncles and aunts were consulted on names. These concepts crossed the Atlantic to survive in the New World. An African model of child discipline, stricter than U.S. standards, prevailed among slaves. This was judged necessary to train new generations in the traditions, skills, and morals vital for survival and for self-respect.

White owners sought to control the naming process and selected babies' names from Greek or Roman history or folklore—Cato, Caesar, or Cupid. To assert their power, masters denied slaves any last names but the masters' own. "It was a crime for a slave to be caught using his own name," wrote Jacob Stroyer.

William Wells Brown "received very severe whippings for telling people that my name was William, after orders were given to change it." But in the slave quarter, said slave Robert Smalls, a ships' pilot who achieved fame in the Civil War, people used their original first and last names.

Laws forbade a husband to raise a hand in defense of himself, his wife, or children. Henry Bibb wrote: "It is useless for a poor slave to resist the white man in a slaveholding state for the law declares that he shall submit or die." To protect each other without risking danger, black women and men had to tread a careful line.

Some defied the risks to fight back. In 1829, a slave named Lydia was shot while defending herself from her master. Judge Ruffin of North Carolina used this case to threaten every slave: "The power of the master must be absolute to render the submission of the slave perfect. The slave, to remain a slave, must be made sensible that there is no appeal from his master."

Moses Grandy escaped to England and dictated his autobiography. He recalled this scene: "I remember well my mother often hid us all in the woods, to prevent master selling us. When we wanted water, she sought for it in any hole or puddle ... full of tadpoles and insects: she strained it, and gave it round to each of us in the hollow of her hand. For food, she gathered berries in the woods, got potatoes, raw corn, etc. After a time the master would send word to her to come in, promising he would not sell us."

Work-weary parents walked long distances to visit families. William Heard's father, who lived three miles away, "would come in on Wednesday nights . . . and be back at his home by daylight, Thursday mornings; come again Saturday night, and return by daylight Monday morning." Heard became a bishop in the African Methodist Episcopal church.

Frederick Douglass told of his mother, who lived twelve miles away, and her "few hasty visits made in the night on foot, after the daily tasks were over, and when she [had to return in time for] the driver's call to the field in early morning." "My pa," recalled a South Carolina slave, "slipped in and out enough times to have four children."

"One of my earliest recollections is that of my mother cooking a chicken late at night, and awakening her children for the purpose of feeding them," said Booker T. Washington. He grew up to become a well-known political figure and educator.

Devotion to family is reflected in slave marriages that outlasted the many disruptions of planter control. Dr. Herbert Gutman's *The Black Family in Slavery and Freedom* states, "Evidence of long marriages is found in all slave settings in the decades preceding the Civil War." His research uncovered that 20,000 North Carolina slaves in seventeen counties and from all classes, at the end of the Civil War, paid a fee of twenty-five cents to register their marriages. In six Virginia counties 2,817 slaves marriages were officially renewed. "No slave family was protected in the law," he wrote, "but upon their emancipation most Virginia ex-slave families had two parents, and most older couples had lived together in long-lasting unions." Among the eager marriage-minded couples were Jacob Wiley, ninety-three, and Phoebe Tanner, eighty, of Davis Bend, Mississippi.

Union officers in the field found the same story of lasting marriage commitments. Commander Thomas Callahan wrote that blacks had "an almost universal anxiety . . . to abide by first connections. Many, both men and women with whom I am acquainted, whose wives or husbands the rebels have driven off, first refuse to form new connections, and declare their purpose to keep faith to absent ones."

At many points women defied the white supremacy system to defend their families. To face down a Georgia slave trader, Harriet Ross hid her boy in a cabin and guarded the door. "You are after my son, but the first man that comes into my house, I will

Black marriage ceremonies marked the end of slavery, some for couples who had been married for decades.

split his head open." When her master's son tried to beat her, she took a pole "and beat him nearly to death with it." Her daughter Harriet saw and learned, and later applied the lessons as Harriet Tubman. Mrs. Ross finally left bondage by mounting a cow and riding away from the plantation in broad daylight.

Other mothers also insisted on teaching daughters to fight. Fannie Jennings of Eden, Tennessee, was vividly remembered by her daughter for her courage. "Ma fussed, fought, and kicked all the time. I tell you, she was a demon. She said she wouldn't be whipped. . . .

"The one doctrine of my mother's teaching which was branded upon my senses was that I should never let anyone abuse me. 'I'll kill you, gal, if you don't stand up for yourself,' she would say. 'Fight, and if you can't fight, kick; if you can't kick, then bite.' Ma was generally willing to work, but if she didn't feel like doing something, none could make her do it."

When some slave owners agreed to let their slaves work for pay, and then use the money to purchase loved ones, many women jumped at the chance. They worked for decades, first to buy their own liberty and then to ransom children and spouses. President Jefferson's servant Alethia Tanner purchased her freedom in 1810, and by 1828 saved enough to buy her sister, ten children, and five grandchildren. In 1836, she bought four more grandchildren. In that year, 476 of Cincinnati's 1,129 free blacks had purchased their own freedom.

Hester Lane, an elderly New Yorker, purchased and then liberated eleven slaves. She began with $100 to buy a young girl she knew from birth, educated her, helped in her marriage and at the births of her four children. Then she bought a boy of fourteen for $200, a man of thirty for $750, a sickly family of three for $140, a woman and her children for $550, and their father for $200. She saw that each child was educated and given a start in business.

Children commonly addressed adults as uncle or aunt. More than a mark of respect, wrote Frederick Douglass, this was a recognition that the young had to be provided for. In Georgia, Aleck was one slave who asked, "Should each man regard only his own children, and forget all the others!" If parents and relatives were traded away or children sold without their parents, men and women without blood ties stepped in to share parenting responsibilities.

The practice of taking in children changed the meaning of the word *parents* in the slave community to mean all adults. " 'Parents' means relations in general . . . family," explained Robert Smalls. A black community expression was, "If you hurt one of the family, you hurt them all."

The African-American tradition of adopting orphans was first noticed by whites after the Civil War. Thomas Conway, director of the Bureau of Free Labor in the gulf states, "thought that five

One of many efforts by the African-American community to protect its young, this orphan asylum began operation in Tennessee during the Civil War.

or ten thousand orphans of the freedmen would be thrown upon our hands at the close of the war, but strange to say, our numbers have hardly increased." He found African-American families gathering "orphaned children of their former friends and neighbors, thus saving us the necessity of bearing large expenses in caring for them."

Even as men and women protected children, owners inflicted a cruel fate on many slave women. To increase the stock of babies for sale, they were bribed and pressured to produce more of them. Tempe Herndon remembered she was prized because "I had so many children." She recalled one master who took young slave women and men and put them in a big barn every Sunday and left them there until Monday morning. She believed sixty babies were born in that way.

Georgia planter John C. Reed said that some masters thought "all day long about the natural increase of slaves." He believed this practice had become the South's "leading industry." The *American Cotton Planter* advised readers to carefully cultivate this "source of great profit to the owner." Rice planter P. C. Weston announced, "Women with six children at any one time are allowed all Saturday to themselves."

Harriet Jacobs recalled what many girls and young women faced: "When she is fourteen or fifteen, her owner or his sons or the overseer or perhaps all of them being able to bribe her with presents. If these fail to accomplish their purpose, she is whipped or starved into submission to their will."

William Craft wrote: "Any man with money . . . can buy a beautiful and virtuous girl." He called it a common practice "for men of the highest circles of society to be the fathers of children by their slaves" and said "the more pious, beautiful, and virtuous the girls are, the greater the price they bring." When prime field hands cost $1,500, some young women sold for $5,000, particularly mixed bloods in New Orleans.

Slavery provided scant protection for women and children.

Whites also invaded black marriages, and battles followed. Josiah Henson remembered his father with "his head bloody and his back lacerated . . . his right ear cut off," because he had beaten the overseer who assaulted his wife. In 1830, in Virginia, a man killed his wife's master because he had kept her locked in a storehouse when she refused him. A Tennessee planter pushed his way into one black marriage bed after another until an irate husband choked the life out of him. In 1859, in Mississippi, Alfred was executed after he killed the overseer who attacked Charlotte, his wife.

Women were also ready to risk death for their marriages. Jarmain Loguen recalled his mother, armed with "all the tiger's blood in her veins" and a heavy stick, striking a knife from a planter's hand, and then knocking him out. A slave named Clarinda swung a hoe that discouraged her master's interest in her, and Cherry Logue swung a club at a man who made "insulting advances."

In Virginia, Sukie punched her owner, who was trying to rip off her dress and throw her to the floor. Sukie managed to push him, seat first, into a pot of boiling soup. He screamed as he ran, but quietly enough so his wife couldn't hear.

Some black women, lured or forced into intimate relationships with whites, used their influence to gain equality and respect. Wives of planters brought suits claiming slave women received the attention, affection, and love they were denied by their husbands. In 1831, in Kentucky, an owner's will was contested by relatives who charged he had been insane. Their proof was he showed "an inclination to marry the slave Grace, whom he liberated."

Some of the resulting interracial marriages brought freedom and equality. Captain Ralph Quarles of Virginia married slave Lucy Langston, then freed her and their three sons. The young men left Virginia for Ohio, one saying, "He did for his sons all

Slaves came in all colors, as this Louisiana family photograph taken during the Civil War shows.

he could in wisdom, in education, and in his will." Poet Langston Hughes was born from this family. Lewis Clarke's sister refused to become the mistress of a man named Coval unless he freed her, and "in about a month he took her to Mexico, emancipated and married her." She and Mr. Coval visited France for a year or more and then the West Indies, and she inherited his fortune.

But most women forced into interracial relationships were unable to do more than hold their pride. One man said his grandmother was raped, but "she carried herself like a queen and was tall and stately."

Louisa Picquet, trapped in a relationship, "had trouble with my soul the whole time," but could only pray for her master's death. When her prayers were answered, she "didn't cry nor nothin', for I was glad he was dead. I was left free, and . . . so glad."

Women field workers found some comfort by singing a song of lament and warning:

> *Rains come wet me,*
> *Sun come dry me.*
> *Stay back, boss man,*
> *Don't come nigh me.*

The exploitation of women and their separation from their men left a bitterness that many could never forget. In 1863, a black couple who had been forced apart, and each of whom had remarried, met in Virginia. The woman felt it was "like a stroke of death to me. We threw ourselves into each other's arms and cried. . . . White folks got a heap to answer for the way they've done to colored folks."

As white fathers and sons sought out black women, their wives hid from the truth. Mistress Mary Chestnut wrote in her diary how "our men live in one house with their wives and their concubines; and the mulattoes one sees in every family partly resemble the white children. Any lady is ready to tell you who is the father of all the mulatto children in everybody's household but her own. Those, she seems to think, drop from the clouds."

Despite repeated assaults, black families tried to reunite. A runaway who fled to Canada in 1853 told his tale of family unity: "My wife got a voucher for her freedom before she would come on. . . . I was in slavery until I was about eighteen years old. There were my four uncles, myself, and mother, and another sister of my uncles. My uncles paid fifteen hundred dollars apiece for themselves. They bought themselves three times. They got cheated out of their freedom in the first instance and were put in jail at one time, and were going to be sold down south, right away; but parties who were well acquainted with us, and knew we had made desperate struggles for freedom, came forward and advanced the money and took us out of jail, and put us on a footing so that we could go ahead and earn money to pay the debt. . . . My uncles bought me, my mother, as well as themselves."

How married love survived separations has been unearthed in recently discovered slave letters. In December 1862, Norfleet, a Texas servant taken with his master into the Confederate army, heard from his wife, Fannie: "I haven't forgotten you nor will I ever forget you as long as the world stands, even if you forget me. My love is as great as it was the first night I married you, and hope it will be so with you. My heart and love is pinned on your breast, and I hope yours is to mine. . . . There is no time night or day but what I am studying about you. . . . Your Loving Wife . . . Fannie."

In the slaves' struggle for knowledge, women, less carefully watched than men, often played a leading role. Whites used to spell out words so blacks couldn't understand what was going on, recalled one woman, "but I ran to uncle and spelled them over to him, and he told me what they meant."

Southern laws imposed harsh penalties for anyone teaching slaves to read or write. Margaret Douglass, a white woman of Norfolk, Virginia, was tried and found guilty, according to the court, "of one of the vilest crimes that ever disgraced society." She had taught Kate, "a slave girl, to read the Bible. No enlightened society can exist where such offenses go unpunished," ruled the court.

During an era when education was a privilege for white men, not women, the African-American community could afford no such distinctions. Some black women daringly conducted secret schools. In Natchez, Louisiana, Milla Granson, who learned to read from the children of her Kentucky master, ran a "midnight school" of twelve pupils each term that taught reading and writing between 11:00 P.M. and 2:00 A.M. She graduated hundreds. Some pupils soon applied their knowledge by writing passes for runaways fleeing to Canada.

Susie King and her younger brother attended an illegal school in Savannah taught by a free black woman, Mrs. Woodhouse. King described the process: "We went every day about nine o'clock, with our books wrapped in paper to prevent the police or white persons from seeing them. We went in, one at a time, through the gate, into the yard to the kitchen, which was the schoolroom. She had twenty-five or thirty children whom she taught, assisted by her daughter, Mary Jane. The neighbors would see us going in sometimes, but they supposed we were there learning trades, as it was the custom to give children a trade of some kind. After school we left the same way we entered, one by one, when we would go to a square, about a block from the school, and wait for each other."

Frederick Douglass first learned to read from his mistress— until her husband found out and exploded "there would be no keeping him. It would forever unfit him to be a slave. He would become unmanageable, and of no value to his master." Douglass had learned more than reading and writing. He understood, as had many black men and women, that on this control of knowledge rested "the white man's power to enslave the black man."

Disrupting Plantation Life

FOUR

On St. Helena Island there is a folk tale of a slave who never had to work. He convinced his master he was disabled and then sat around strumming his guitar and singing, "I was fooling my master seventy-two years, and I'm fooling him now." Master and slave shared the same land, but not the same values or even the same sense of humor.

One exasperated slaveholder said, "I'm nearly worried to death with them—if I had a jail, I should lock them up every night."

Plantation owners and overseers found their working days were an unending battle of wits. Despite whips, guns, and unlimited power, they did not always win. John W. Brown complained his slaves "have wearied out all the patience I had with them now for nine years." Even nightfall did not bring relaxation and sleep. A visitor to the South reported: "I have known times here when not a single planter had a calm night's rest. They never lie down to sleep without . . . loaded pistols at their sides."

Frederick Douglass believed both owner and slave were victims of the system. He said, "Reason is imprisoned here and passions run wild." Douglass's cousin, an attractive young woman, was sexually abused by Plummer, her overseer. When she protested to her owner, known for his kindness, he beat her. Douglass coldly concluded: "The treatment was part of the system rather than part of the man. To have encouraged appeals of this kind would have occasioned much loss of time, and leave the overseer powerless to enforce obedience."

The leather whip singing in the air, bringing blood from a black back, was the usual answer to any resistance, real or imagined. Howard C. Bruce, who escaped to write a book about his adventures, said slaves "took no interest in their master's work . . . and went no further than forced by the lash."

"I find Robert a very hard hand to manage," said Senator John Hammond. "I have flogged him until I'm tired."

Senator Alexander Stephens jailed his slave Pierce, but his overseer reported "his imprisonment had only tended to harden him. . . . I don't think he will ever conform."

John's owner had the young slave "heavily ironed and put to work," but had "given up all hope of ever being able to make him an honest and obedient boy, whippin' does no good, and advice is nearly thrown away."

To keep control, owners tried hard to divide their laborers. "They taught us to be against one another and no matter where you would go you would always find one that would tattle and have the white folks pecking on you," recalled a slave woman. Planter Knott offered five dollars for those willing to betray their people, saying, "I always like to encourage negroes in betraying runaways."

House servants were treated better than field hands, light-skinned individuals better than dark, and women better than men, in the hope favored individuals would pass on news heard in the slave quarter. African-American communities had to learn to screen out unreliable members, and to deal with informers.

Robust black men were selected as drivers and given whip power over field hands. If they failed to carry out orders, they were flogged. Solomon Northup, a Louisiana driver for eight years, devised a clever response. He threw "the lash within a hair's breadth of the back of the ear or the nose, without, however, touching either of them." When overseers appeared, Northup's laborers helped in the drama with a "squirm and screech as if in agony."

Patrols, or "pattyrollers" as they were called by the African-American community, roamed the countryside at night. They checked to be sure slaves were in their houses and to see if those who were out had passes from a white person. They were known for savage brutality, particularly when they encountered groups of slaves at secret religious or other meetings. Black people tried to avoid them, and sometimes set traps for their horses or burned their homes.

The spirit of resistance showed many faces. Slave patrols examine passes of slaves out after dark.

1. Since their labor was stolen, slaves justified, and counted as a form of resistance, stealing from slaveholders. A woman found with her mistress's trinkets said, "Don't say I'm wicked . . . it's all right for us poor colored people to appropriate whatever of the white folks' blessings the Lord puts in our way."

Planter Thomas Chaplin complained of "my little rascal William, who I had minding the crows off the watermelons." But William "had been the worst crow himself, and does the thing quite systemmatically. . . . Cunning, very."

In the field, black women and men found a variety of ways of fooling whites or disturbing production. Reporter Olmsted observed what whites called eye-service—work performed only when slaves were watched. Against strict orders, gates were left open and bars let down, rails removed from fences, mules injured, tools broken. Everywhere was careless workmanship, boats left to drift away, heavy items moved, dangerous embankment holes not filled but thinly patched on top. Workers failed to perform jobs and then lied.

2. One owner told Olmsted slaves "never did a fair day's work. They could not be made to work hard; they never would lay out their strength freely, and it was impossible to make them do it." Planters also found that almost anything used in production could be ruined. There were mysteriously bent hoes, broken plows, toothless rakes, and injured field animals. Howard Bruce told how slaves deliberately overworked field animals and plowed too shallow for planting of crops. Slave sabotage was so widespread that planters invented a thick "slave hoe" that could not easily be broken. Many planters feared to introduce the plow. Mules, harder to injure than horses, were often used.

3. Production on some plantations varied as much as 100 percent due to slowdowns and sabotage. Slaves pretended to be too sick or lame to work, women pretended they were pregnant, and illness soared when work was hardest. In Mississippi, the

Wheeles plantation calculated one working day each week was lost by sickness. The Bowles plantation found that of 159 days lost due to sickness, only 5 were on Sunday, a day of rest. One planter found that a man he considered too blind to work in the field made "eighteen good crops for himself when the [Civil] war was over."

4. Strikes, slowdowns, or what owners called "the danger of a general stampede to the swamp" were common. One manager told reporter Olmsted slaves ran away to protest overseers and harsh working conditions: "They hide in the swamp and come into the cabins at night to get food." Some lengthy stoppages were only settled when owners agreed to negotiate with their slaves.

Escapes to the swamps and to visit relatives marked the history of American slavery.

A few slaves devised a special revenge on owners during a sale or auction. Pretending to be sick, insane, or disabled, their stumbling or incoherent manner wrecked sales, drove away buyers, or brought lower prices. One light-skinned slave claimed to have escaped during negotiations for his sale. He said he talked faster than his darker-skinned master and sold the white man instead. With the cash he made his way north.

Overseers, often known for their abusiveness, did not have a happy time, and some had to fight for their lives. In rural Alabama Olmsted was told: "The overseers have to always go about armed; their life wouldn't be safe, if they didn't. As it is, they very often get cut pretty bad."

Cudjo Lewis was busy working in the field when he saw a group of women overpower and "soundly thrash" an overseer who had insulted one of them.

In 1853, one Alabama overseer was wounded when slaves rebelled. He finally put down the uprising, but since little blood was shed and no lives were lost, he only imposed a token punishment on the rebels.

Though direct challenges to work rules could be suicidal, some slaves spoke up. Beverly Jones recalled Jake, who told his Virginia master, "You can sell me, lash me, or kill me. I ain't caring which, but you can't make me work no more." The owner thought for a moment and said, "All right, Jake. I'm retiring you, but for God's sake don't say anything to the other niggers."

At times, slowdowns or protests forced changes. Masters might fire overseers in constant combat with their workers, especially if production fell. Some agreed to compromise with their slaves, one promising his overseer would ask "nothing unreasonable" from them. A Virginia master found his "overseer lacks authority among the Negroes, to make up for which he is very industrious and works with them."

Frederick Douglass learned early that the slave whipped easiest is whipped most. Sent to a slave-breaker named Edward Covey,

Young Frederick Douglass was sent to "slave-breaker" Edward Covey. Douglass turned on Covey and beat him in a fair fight. This drawing is from 1853.

who tried to beat him into submission, young Douglass finally lost his temper. A "fighting madness had come upon me," and he found himself in a dangerous wrestling match. "I was strictly on the defensive, preventing him from injuring me, rather than trying to injure him. I flung him on the ground several times . . . I held him firmly by the throat, that his blood followed my nails." Douglass clobbered a cousin of Covey who rushed to the rescue and warned away a hired man and a slave woman Covey had called. Douglass battled Covey for two hours until the slave-breaker gave up. Covey announced he "whipped" Douglass, but never bothered him again.

A somewhat less hazardous form of resistance, fire, began early and burned late throughout the slave era. Arson was a quick, powerful form of retribution, which could be used selectively and could leave enough time for those with the matches to flee. On the Pierce Butler plantation Fanny Kemble reported field hands made fires to cook their meals "and sometimes through their careless neglect, but sometimes, too, undoubtedly on purpose, the woods are set fire to."

"Fires are continually occurring in this country," reported a visitor to Georgia.

From colonial times, whites claimed slaves were busy setting fires. In 1741, two Hackensack, New Jersey, slaves were executed for starting fires. In 1766, a Maryland woman was executed for burning down her master's home, tobacco house, and outbuildings. In 1781, a Virginia resident wrote of "most alarming times this summer" as blacks burned homes.

By the 1790s, Charleston citizens organized to see if brick and stone instead of wood could be used for building homes. By the next century most Virginia homes had fire escapes, and visitor Morris Birkbeck noted "many whites [have] an extraordinary fear" of fires due to the "carelessness of the negroes."

The turmoil during the War of 1812 led to new opportunities for arsonists. The *Norfolk Herald* reported "four negroes in the jail . . . committed as incendiaries." It wrote: "The danger to be apprehended to our town from an attack of the enemy is safety to what is to be apprehended from the lurking incendiary." By 1820, the American Fire Insurance Company of Philadelphia announced it "declined making insurances in any of the slave states." In 1831, Richmond businesses feared goods destroyed by fire "would not be paid by insurers."

Some arsonists struck at hated pattyrollers. In 1830, a southern report said some pattyrollers had quit and other "patrols are of no service" after two "had their dwelling houses and other houses burnt down." In 1852, Princess Anne County, Virginia, patrollers, who had just dispersed a black meeting, suddenly had to race from one blazing pattyroller home to another.

If fire was a favorite general terror weapon, poison was the favorite lethal choice against individuals. Women, especially those who were nurses and cooks with easy access to medical supplies, were often charged in poison plots. Some were accused of bringing a knowledge of lethal formulas from Africa.

In 1740, New York City's two thousand African Americans were accused of trying to poison the water supply for ten thousand whites. Whites who could afford it bought spring water from vendors.

In 1751, South Carolina demanded the death penalty for blacks who poisoned whites, and "for any black who instructed another black in the knowledge of any poisonous root, plant, herb, or other poison." Ten years later the *Charleston Gazette* announced: "The negroes have again begun the hellish practice of poisoning." In 1755, Maryland convicted five slaves and Virginia two slaves for conspiring to poison whites. By 1770, Georgia provided a death penalty, saying poisoning has "frequently been committed by slaves." In 1805, when two respected whites were poisoned, a conspiracy charge was brought against nineteen black men and one woman in three North Carolina counties.

Other women also joined men in plantation resistance. In December 1774, the *Georgia Gazette* reported four slave women and four men on a rampage "killed an overseer in the field . . . murdered his wife, and dangerously wounded a carpenter." In 1822, owner Levin Adams described a slim, six-foot runaway: "Sarah is the biggest devil that ever lived, having poisoned a stud horse and set a stable on fire, also burnt G. R. Williams stable and stockyard with seven horses and other property to the value of $1,500. She was handcuffed and got away at Ruddles Mills on her way down the river, which is the fifth time she escaped."

From colonial times on, many planters complained their slaves were "running amok." This often meant that white control had

Black runaways battle whites in a barn.

broken down. In 1773, Robin on the Carter plantation in Virginia not only ran away, but was "destroying corn in the fields." One master wrote about how he had "narrowly escaped being murdered by two of his most trusty negroes," and a paper reported William Allen of Charleston "was chopped to pieces in his barn."

Louisiana whites felt matters were getting out of hand in 1850. One report told of a slave who "broke open and robbed Mrs. Black's house and was very insolent to her." At the Magruder plantation slaves rode into the yard on horseback, baked biscuits in the main house, took a bundle of bread, and went back home to bed.

Favorite servants in the main house showed a gritty impudence. Alcey, a talented cook on the Smedes' Mississippi plantation, wanted a transfer to the fields. According to Susan Dabney Smedes, Alcey "systematically disobeyed orders and stole or destroyed the greater part of the provisions given to her for the table. No special notice was taken, so she resolved to show more plainly that she was tired of the kitchen. Instead of getting the chickens for dinner from the coop, as usual, she unearthed from some corner an old hen that had been sitting for weeks, and [when company was invited to dinner] served her up as a fricassee." The next day she was allowed to march off to the field.

Robert Falls, who felt badly about always having to scrape and bow before his master, swore, "If I had my life to live over, I would die fighting rather than be a slave again." His father, he recalled, "was a fighter. He was mean as a bear. He was so bad to fight and so troublesome he was sold four times to my knowing and maybe a heap more times." In the father and son in the Falls family can be seen two very different responses to bondage—and the fearsome price resisters paid for their courage.

During the Civil War, as slaves deserted the plantation, one South Carolina planter realized their true feelings. "We are all laboring under a delusion. I believed that these people were content, happy, and attached to their masters. But events and recollection have caused me to change these opinions. . . . If they were content, happy, and attached to their masters, why did they desert him in the moment of his need and flock to an enemy, whom they did not know; and thus left their perhaps really good masters whom they did know from infancy."

To planter Frederick A. Eustis the realization came when he returned a year after the war to his home on the Georgia Sea Islands. He found his ex-slaves at work. "I never knew, during forty years of plantation life, so little sickness. Formerly, every man had fever of some kind, and now the veriest old cripple, who did nothing under secesh rule, will row a boat three nights in succession to Edisto [Island], or will pick up the corn about the corn house. There are twenty people whom I know who were considered worn out and too old to work under the slave system who are now working cotton as well as their two acres of provisions; and their crops look very well."

"Shamming," said one owner, "slaves are famous for it." But many masters such as Eustis learned of their deception too late.

Industrial and Urban Resistance

FIVE

Slave labor did far more than bring in southern crops. In 1795, Irish visitor Isaac Weld found slaveholders "have nearly everything they can want on their estates," and that African Americans filled the skilled positions as "taylors, shoemakers, carpenters, smiths, turners, wheelwrights, weavers, tanners."

Slaves built George Washington's Mount Vernon and Thomas Jefferson's Monticello. They constructed the famous iron-grill balconies of New Orleans, built churches, jails, and the beautiful Touro Synagogue in Newport, Rhode Island.

Slaves were managers of plantations and rice mills, and a few were architects, civil engineers, and inventors. Their contribution stimulated a growing U.S. economy. One slave is credited with helping Eli Whitney invent the cotton gin, and another with helping Cyrus McCormick create the reaper. Slave Benjamin Bradley created a steam-engine model out of a gun barrel, pewter, and round pieces of steel, sold it, and used the cash to build an engine large enough to propel a battleship. Bradley became an inventor for the U.S. Naval Academy at Annapolis.

Slave laborers cleared wilderness land and built log cabins. They piloted steamboats, ferries, and early locomotives. Some dug gold in California and others roped and branded cattle from South Carolina to Texas. Their labor built bridges in Mississippi, hotels in Alabama, roads in Louisiana, and ships in Georgia and Maryland. The Norfolk ferryboat was run by a slave pilot, engineer, and crew, and ten thousand others ran Ohio and Mississippi River steamboats.

Slaves were lead miners in Virginia and Missouri, salt miners in Kentucky, Alabama, and Virginia, lumber workers from Texas to Virginia, ironworkers in Virginia and South Carolina, and turpentine producers in North Carolina and Alabama. They built southern canals, railroads, tunnels, ships, turnpikes, and worked for gas and light companies. They labored for U.S. Army and federal government projects in the southern states.

Some became managers. Sandy Maybank, head carpenter at the Reverend C. C. Jones's rice mill and plantation, was placed in charge when Jones was away. Horace, slave architect and civil engineer, built bridges for Robert Jemison, Jr., a wealthy Alabama manufacturer. His owner and Jemison had the 1845 legislature emancipate Horace, and the three continued their business partnership and personal relationship.

The southern iron industry depended on 10,000 slave laborers. The Oxford Iron Works in Virginia owned 220 slaves, the Nesbitt Manufacturing Company of South Carolina used 120, and the giant Tredager Iron Company of Virginia had 450 slaves working alongside an equal number of whites. The Statue of Freedom for the Capitol dome in Washington was bolted together and finally lifted into place, reported the *New York Tribune,* by a "black master builder," who had replaced the white who went on strike. Roads westward were often clogged with skilled whites unable to compete with slave labor.

Half a million slaves lived and worked in southern cities by the 1850s. Blacks made up half of Charleston's population. Some 70,000 lived in the region's eight leading urban centers, and their numbers were expanding rapidly in Mobile, Savannah, Montgomery, and Richmond. Most were men, more likely than women to be taught urban and industrial skills, but women were represented in occupations such as cooks, maids, and servants.

Slaves were part of city life in Baltimore.

Urban slavery was not the half-freedom some whites claimed. An urban escapee denied it was not hard and insisted, "Slavery is *Slavery*, wherever it is found." Urban working hours sometimes exceeded twelve or even sixteen hours a day, and sugar refineries reached eighteen hours a day, "day and night, except during the winter months," reported an overseer. One sugar mill did not grant slaves the Christmas and New Year's holidays for four out of five years in the 1850s. This also happened in other refineries.

In cities, slaves found dangerous work, poor living quarters, and inadequate clothing. The owner of the Oxford Iron Works said he "supplied what I consider absolutely necessary for his health & endurance." Slave eating conditions at a rice mill were described by a white observer: "Chairs, tables, plates, knives, forks, they had none; they sat on the earth or doorsteps, and ate either out of their little cedar tubs or an iron pot, some few with broken iron spoons, more with pieces of wood, and all the children with their fingers."

Urban slaves were not allowed to stroll through city streets when they wished, and some were locked in day and night. When outside, they had to wear badges or carry employer passes. The New Orleans Gas Company built fifteen-foot brick walls and iron gates between their fifty bondsmen and the sparkling nightlife of New Orleans. "The whole of our concern is surrounded with a brick wall ten feet high," said an Alabama textile manager, and "no one is admitted after work hours except the watchman or one of the owners."

Whites wished they could have sealed off the slaves from the quarter of a million free people of color who lived in southern cities. Slavery was a society built for master and slave, and a free black, complained white Charlestonians in 1822, "excites our slaves, who continually have before their eyes persons of the same color, many of whom they had known in slavery . . . freed from the control of masters, working where they please, going whither they please." Seeing them, "the slave pants for freedom." Though carefully watched lest they help fugitives and hounded by legal restrictions, some opened their homes to runaways—sisters, brothers, and perfect strangers.

In Baltimore, slave Frederick Douglass learned the animosity white workers felt toward blacks. Employed as a caulker in a shipyard, he was attacked by whites fearful that blacks might take their jobs. Assaulted by a white who challenged his right to work, Douglass "threw him into the dock. Whenever any of them struck me, I struck back again, regardless of consequences." But he was finally attacked by four at once who "came near killing me, in broad daylight."

He reported the incident to his owner, whose indignation, Douglass found, "resulted from the thought that his rights of property, in my person, had not been respected, more than from any sense of outrage committed on me as a man." Owner and slave appeared before Judge Watson for an arrest warrant, but since no white witnesses testified for Douglass, none was issued.

Whites were deeply divided over employing slaves in cities or industries. Slaveholders spent time and money training slaves in skills with the hope of renting them out. But a group of Charlestonians declared their city's slaves were "in every way . . . conducting themselves as if they were not slaves." Another white warned city slaves "get strange notions in their heads and grow discontented."

James Stirling toured urban and rural regions and wrote his *Letters from the Slave States* (1857). To him the South was "one of her own cotton-steamers," filled from hold to topdeck "with the most inflammable matter," "everything heated to the burning point," a stiff wind blowing from one end to the other, her "high pressure boiler . . . pressed to bursting." "On such a volcano is based the institution of slavery," wrote Stirling. The slaveholder remedy was repression, but Stirling's view was different: "Ter-

Frederick Douglass fled slavery in Baltimore to become a world-famous antislavery lecturer and author. Here he speaks before a British audience.

rorism does not pacify a people. It only changes complaint to conspiracy."

If the whites were divided over black laborers in their cities, slaves were united in their preference for urban work over the dull plantation routines. In cities many could find ways to earn extra money to gain freedom and purchase loved ones. Emanuel Quivers, hired out to the Tredager Iron Company, persuaded its owner to buy him. After four years of laboring for wages he purchased himself, his wife, and four children. The Quivers family settled in Gold Rush California, where the children gained an education and one became foreman in a Stockton factory.

Though they had escaped from plantation routines, slaves still revolted against their urban masters and urban routines, excessive confinement, work hazards, and demanding overseers and bosses. Like rural laborers they slowed efforts to a crawl, feigned sickness, stole or sabotaged equipment and property, set fires, challenged bosses in many overt and covert ways, and conspired at insurrections or flights to freedom.

James's overseer complained about his cobbler, "He will not do what is proper . . . he is capable of finishing six pairs of shoes a week and he seldom does more than three." Jack in an Alabama coal mine refused to pump water and instead "lay there on a plank and went to sleep insisting that it was not necessary to haul anymore," said the manager.

The master of Jack Savage faced a clever, resistant young man. He found Savage "exceedingly lazy, quite smart . . . always giving trouble" and "capable of murdering me, or burning my dwelling at night."

Some slaves refused to handle dangerous factory jobs and others failed to return after Christmas season. Complaining of beatings, lack of food, overwork, and having to wash their own clothes on Sunday, slaves for a railroad contractor stopped work. In many factories slave sickness was so common bosses could not tell when men were ill or faking.

Sabotage took some unusual turns among skilled industrial slaves. Two black railroad workers, seeing an oncoming, roaring locomotive, jumped off their handcar without telling the overseer riding with them. An overseer in a sugar mill so outraged one slave, he tried to push the white man into the boiling juice.

As hired workers, slaves resented sweating for someone else's gain—a person who was not even their owner. Anthony, told to work on Sunday by a furnace manager, said Sunday was "his day and that he was not going to take it up going to your place," and the two had a fight.

Jordan Hatcher, seventeen, scuffled with his Virginia boss. He finally fled after striking the man fatally with a poker. Captured, he was sentenced to death, but his sentence was commuted by Virginia's governor.

Theft became a common way of expressing resentment, helping oneself, or halting production. Manufacturer William Weaver complained, "I'm afraid if I leave here they will steal the place. They come very near it while I am here."

Jacob, a blacksmith, made himself a key to steal provisions from a smokehouse. Frank, a carpenter, stole $160 in gold and silver from his master, also using a key he had made.

To insure production, some masters provided both attractive rewards and fearful punishments. Food and clothing allowances were increased for hard workers, held back from those who failed to meet quotas. In 1857, a gristmiller decided: "Don't give John & Charles any summer shoes, because they killed a goat." Time off at Christmas was either cut or extended for certain slaves depending on the employer's views of their efficiency and proper behavior.

Overtime pay, called "stimulant and reward money," was commonly used to increase slave production in factories. For working on Sundays, a tobacco manufacturer paid slaves one to three dollars a week. One boss paid his men extra cash, calling it "nothing more nor less than presents for their good behavior while working." The Savannah fire department welcomed and paid slaves extra cash for fighting fires, or being among the first to reach a blazing home or business.

A Lexington, Kentucky, rope factory employer argued for the system of stimulant and reward money: "This keeps them contented and makes them ambitious, and more labor is obtained . . . than could possibly be forced from them by severity." But a Lexington visitor to a hemp factory found another hand behind the plan: "The stimulus of wages is applied behind the whip, of course the prime motor."

Reporter Olmsted talked with an urban capitalist whose complaints sounded like those of rural planters. "We have tried reward and punishments, but it makes no difference. . . . We must always calculate that they will not labor at all except to avoid punishment, and they will never do more than just enough to save themselves from being punished, and no amount of punishment will prevent their working carelessly and indifferently."

The use of arson as a slave weapon leaped from farm to city. Useful because it was easily available and hard to pin on a fast-moving suspect, it gave employers of slaves one more worry. In 1845, Senator Henry Clay's Lexington bagging factory burned down mysteriously. A Texas employer claimed his blacksmith burned down his shop and a court agreed. One slave stepped up and told his master he would burn down his factory if the overseer was not fired.

The surprise and shock when "the most trusted," "faithful," and privileged slaves ran away had become a southern white tradition. This dismay thrived in urban as well as rural settings, among skilled and factory slaves as well as field hands.

Most left their workbenches to stay with nearby relatives. They fled for a few days or a week and returned after visiting loved ones. A common cause for flight came when slaves heard they were about to be punished, or sold away from family. Absenteeism also peaked in some factories during late summer and fall when production pressures soared.

Often slaves tried to handle the issue of visits to wives or loved ones by honest bargaining. Some even offered to make up lost time. But when turned down, some just disappeared to return later. In one instance, six men asked for a leave, were turned down, and argued for weeks with the overseer of a river improvement project. When he still refused, they picked up and left. The overseer, to head off a complete breakdown of his authority, hastily decided to let the rest visit their wives.

Slaves found new opportunities for flight from cities, especially ports or rail depots. A great advantage was the number of free blacks and friendly whites who might write passes and provide cash, directions, or other help. One black Louisiana carpenter sold forged passes for runaways. Although officials seized him, he escaped with one of his passes.

Manuel, a slave, bought a certificate of freedom from a friend, reached Philadelphia under another name, and persuaded an abolitionist to purchase his children. Some fugitives took jobs as sailors and then jumped ship at ports from Liverpool, England, to Boston and Detroit. Frederick Douglass left his caulker job in a Baltimore shipyard and fled to New York City with a pass forged by a black seaman.

A southern city could not tolerate a peaceful protest by African Americans. On a hot July day in 1853, John Scott and twenty-two other slaves marched to the Richmond mayor's office to demand the facts about a will they believed freed 118 people. Scott, speaking for the twenty-two men and women, almost half of whom had learned to read and write, said their intention was to return to "the home of our forefathers in Africa." The delegation was arrested, but Scott again insisted "we cannot be still until we get home to Africa."

Whites in southern cities, despite their many efforts at slave control, never felt completely secure. Urban slaves and free blacks played a leading role in the largest slave plots and rebellions of the nineteenth century, as we shall see in Chapter 9. In 1856, industrial slaves—Louisiana sugar millers, Arkansas salt boilers, Missouri lead and iron miners, particularly along the Cumberland River—were found conspiring for freedom. Scores were arrested and twenty-nine were executed.

The next year, Dred Scott, a St. Louis slave, made history. Because his master took him to the Wisconsin Territory where slavery was banned, Scott said he and his family were free. In St. Louis he hired attorneys and began a lawsuit that lasted more than a decade.

In 1857, the Supreme Court by a seven-to-two vote turned down the Scott family's plea for liberty. The High Court decision made it legal for slaveholders to bring their slave property to any state and territory in the United States and added that a black "had no rights which the white man was bound to respect." It was not known at the time that president-elect James Buchanan, in violation of the Constitution's separation of powers, had intervened by sending letters on his views to three Supreme Court justices.

However, by that time, the family had an owner who liberated them. The Scotts remained in St. Louis, where Dred worked as a porter at Barnum's Hotel and also helped his wife, Harriet, run a laundry business. Tourists came to see the hotel porter whose case helped push the United States toward civil war.

Years of toil had ruined the Scotts' health, and in 1858 Dred Scott died of tuberculosis. The next year Harriet Scott died. But the elderly couple, who fought so doggedly for liberty, died as free people.

Music for Jesus, Lyrics of Freedom

SIX

As he visited the campfires of his black troops during the Civil War, Colonel Thomas Wentworth Higginson was startled by the "flower of poetry" and potency of their songs. He found time to write down lyrics for three dozen songs that "were to the men more than a source of relaxation; they were a stimulus to courage and a tie to heaven." Behind the gentle words in praise of God lurked the spiritual armor of people long at war with oppression.

After the war the Reverend Mr. Higginson published his notes and tried to describe the gripping power and meaning of the melodies he had heard. The music that captivated Higginson later conquered the world stage . . . as the blues, jazz, and rock.

These songs from the battlefield were unlike any other American music. The white Protestant hymns and evangelical melodies of the day did not approach the complex rhythms, syncopation, and particularly the call and response and spontaneity of African-American music. Soloists sang a dialogue with or blended into a chorus that represented the congregation. Together, they created intricate patterns Europeans never tried.

Lacking training in European music, Africans were not bound by its structure and restrictions. Flexible voices casually altered lyrics and sounds to produce what one critic called "an improvisational communal consciousness." In 1845, a white traveler wrote: "The blacks themselves leave out old stanzas and introduce new ones at pleasure. Traveling through the South, you may, in passing from Virginia to Louisiana, hear the same tune a hundred times, but seldom the same words accompanying it."

Beginning with the banning of the drum as an instrument of communication, slaveholders tried to set boundaries for African culture. But the songs, folk tales, and religious experience of African Americans demonstrated that masters could never stifle black vitality, creativity, and community. The words and music

Drums (basic to African communication), music, and dance were banned in the Americas.

of black songs not only lifted spirits and ignited hope, but sounded a call to a bright new day. The stark, haunting beauty of slave songs conveyed an immediate sense of community sharing and expression and bonded individuals with neighbors.

It is one of history's great ironies that Christianity, the Bible, and the words of Christ would eagerly be grasped by both slaves and slaveholders. For one, religion, the Book, and the words justified a profitable system. For the other, they would cast a curse on bondage and offer faith in deliverance from tears and chains. Over the meaning of Christianity, slave and master carried on a political debate about liberty and justice.

Africans first met evangelical Christians as captors on the slave ships of the Atlantic. In the Americas, Protestant ministers called the Africans heathens in need of salvation and began the process of conversion. Hoping Christian baptism might lead to liberty or an easing of slavery's burdens, African Americans embraced the unfamiliar divinities. Worried lest a black stampede to church might undermine the system, in the seventeenth century a Virginia court ruled "baptisme of slaves doth not exempt them from bondage."

Those in chains found in Christian spirit both inspiration and solace during a life of bondage. In the Bible, African Americans found a God who favored retribution, a Jesus who died to save humanity, and a Moses who led Hebrew people out of slavery. Surrounded by white demons and separated from home by a three-thousand-mile ocean, African Americans prayed their caring God might again part the waves of the Red Sea for his chosen people.

Owners approached conversion of their slaves with distinct goals. They aimed to turn resistance to docility and replace flight and sabotage with increased production. Laborers would be taught to obey masters and overseers and seek justice in heaven. To this end, the Bible and Christian worship were shaped into a propaganda for conformity.

Some whites doubted that Christian teachings could reform blacks, and others resented the cost and time of this religious experiment. How would slave congregations interpret Baptist and Methodist messages of spiritual equality? Would instruction in Christian piety and ethics raise questions about slaveholders being entitled to enter heaven? Could Christianity in the hands of the oppressed prove a double-edged sword? These nagging questions were debated among whites until emancipation.

But an enthusiastic faith in Christianity carried the day. A rebellious, obstinate race, it argued, would become obedient servants. A savage people would be filled with awe of God and respect for his earthly rulers. To insure success for their gospel, masters selected trusted ministers, and laws required whites be present at all religious gatherings.

Though Christianity was encouraged among slaves, religious meetings were supervised by the planter and his family.

In Latin America, a powerful Catholic Church pressured slave owners and governments and finally won reforms. In the United States, a Protestant church fragmented into many separate denominations proved too weak to challenge the South's powerful ruling class. Slaveholders paid the local clergy and commanded their obedience. The few pious men of God who questioned the gospel of slavery were soon silenced, fired, or driven away.

In Bishop Meade's sermons, slaveholders found the dogma they sought. He urged black congregants, "Do all service for . . . your masters and mistresses here on earth . . . as if you did it for God himself." The bishop said God was the highest slaveholder:

> Poor creatures! You little consider, when you are idle and neglectful of your master's business, when you steal, and waste, and hurt any of their substance, when you are saucy and impudent, when you are telling lies and deceiving them, or when you prove stubborn and sullen, and will not do the work you are set about without stripes and vexation—you do not consider, I say, that what faults you are guilty of towards your masters and mistresses are faults done against God himself, who hath set your masters and mistresses over you in His own stead, and expects that you would do for them just as you would do for him. And pray do not think that I want to deceive you when I tell you that your masters and mistresses are God's overseers, and that, if you are faulty towards them, God himself will punish you severely for it in the next world.

Whites wanted to believe their version of the gospel was having its desired impact on the African-American community. Advertisements for sales and auctions stressed the "Christian character" of the slaves—suggesting they were cowed, docile servants who would never flee from, lie to, or reject white orders. Frederick Douglass met many slaves "who are under the delusion that God required them to submit to slavery and to wear their chains with meekness and humility."

Others challenged the new ideas. "This is the way it go," recalled Wes Turner of Virginia. "Be nice to massa an' missus; don't be mean; be obedient, and work hard. That was all the Sunday school lesson they taught."

John Thompson angrily described ministers he heard as "God in the face, and the Devil in the heart." Submission to God was one thing, said a slave mother, but "submission to the machinations of Satan was quite another."

Most slaves still enjoyed their time in church as a relief from work, offering cultural and religious satisfactions. Some congregants dared to challenge white ministers. Beverly Jones told how an Uncle Silas stood up and asked Preacher Johnson of Virginia, "Is us slaves gonna be free in heaven?" When the preacher refused to respond, Uncle Silas stood and repeated his question again and again. After that service Uncle Silas never returned to church.

African-American Christianity demanded its own gospel, and many slave communities began their own secret churches. There Christianity was interpreted not by white preachers but by congregations. One slave remembered: "When they wanted to sing and pray, they would steal off into the woods. . . . Whipping did not stop them from having meetings. When one place was located, they would find another." Some groups just found "a thicket to hide in and pray for deliverance."

Masters feared the spread of this independent Christian worship and dispatched the dreaded pattyrollers to break up meetings. Posses scoured the countryside searching for illegal worship services, looking for trouble and hoping for violence. Wes Turner told how his flock ran grapevines across paths to trip mounted pattyrollers. A white patrol finally located and attacked Turner and his church in the woods. A patroller yelled, "You

African Americans sought to keep their heritage despite the efforts of slaveholders to eradicate African music, drums, and dance.

ain't got no time to serve God. We bought you to serve us."

Many congregations managed to survive assaults and reopen churches. The Bible continued to breathe strength into their struggle and to lift their daily burdens. Their hymns were rarely sorrowful or tearful, for they had to raise spirits.

The most common lyrical image selected by African-American congregations was that of "the chosen people"—a celebration of pride, survival, and humanity. Congregations composed such lyrics as "We are the people of God," "The people that is born of God," and "We are the people of the Lord." Away from the ears of their enemies, people told of slaveholders who could not reach heaven, but "To the promised land I'm bound to go."

Despite the walls erected by their masters, African Americans creatively employed religion, song, and story to tear at the chains that bound them. Biblical heroes and a world struggle for liberty masked the real theme of a coming day of liberation.

Much as African Americans shaped the music of the New World, they recast the European's abstract, severe God. Recent scholars have pointed out that African Americans converted God rather than converted to Him. The God worshiped in black churches was as immediate as the gods of Africa.

Biblical characters became intimate, personal friends or close relatives. One African-American song proclaimed, "Jesus is my bosom friend," another announced, "I'm going to talk with King Jesus by myself," and still others told about warm, friendly kin-folk—"Sister Mary," "Brother Moses," and "Brother Daniel."

This personal God, committed to justice, was willing to drown the pharaoh's army of slaveholders to save the Hebrew children. So powerful a friend was bound to help his devout followers who had been forced to walk the earth in chains. African Americans sang the praises of a Jesus who could be counted on:

> *Gwine to write to Mass Jesus,*
> *To Send some Valiant soldier*
> *To turn back Pharaoh's army, Hallelu!*

God and Jesus were portrayed as leaders on freedom's battle-field.

That was exactly what masters were worried about. As early as 1810, planter Richard Byrd of Virginia informed the governor that "slave preachers used their religious meetings as veils for revolutionary schemes." To carry forth a Christianity that pro-vided slaves real comfort and support—and yet avoided trigger-ing white fury—black preachers carefully constructed sermons, tales, and lyrics that sounded innocent to white ears.

The theme of revolutionary change appeared in spirituals as scriptural references. Were congregations saluting the Holy Spirit or talking treason? Samson threatens, "If I had my way, I'd tear the building down." A spiritual about God's powerful voice ringing through heaven and hell concludes: "My dungeon shook and my chains, they fell." Was the past or future being celebrated? Masters and their handpicked clergymen tried to fasten slaves' attention on heaven's glory rather than today's plight. Black theology invariably preached messages of deliverance.

Some whites warned a militant Christianity could lead slaves astray, even toward rebellion. Slave plots often involved, as did an 1816 conspiracy in Camden, South Carolina, respected church members. The famous leaders of nineteenth-century insurrections, Gabriel Prosser, Denmark Vesey, and Nat Turner, were devout Christians convinced their rage to rebel was divinely inspired. Vesey's plan, recalled one of the conspirators, was "about religion, which he would apply to slavery."

Another witness testified Vesey "read to us from the Bible, how the children of Israel were delivered out of Egypt from bondage." He felt it was imperative to "attempt their emancipation however shocking and bloody might be the consequences." "Retribution," Vesey stressed, would be "pleasing to the Almighty."

In Virginia, Nat Turner, a popular lay preacher, said a black, avenging Messiah appeared in a dream to call him to action. God told him to "fight against the Serpeant, for the time was fast approaching when the first should be last and the last should be first." After Turner's defeat, legislatures made slave preaching illegal. "No black man ought to be permitted to turn a preacher through the country," the *Richmond Enquirer* warned.

Christian doctrine and devotion to liberty remained intertwined in slave hearts long after Turner's time. In 1839, Mississippians heard many rumors of slave plots, and "suspicion centered around the 'itinerant preachers,' " reported an official. The next year New Orleans papers complained about a black church it called a "den for hatching plots against masters." Seven years later twelve black worshipers were arrested by police and charged with "singing hymns . . . followed by sermons [of] the most inflammatory character."

✳ Christianity inspired Harriet Tubman, hero of the Underground Railroad and liberator of three hundred slaves, who said, "I must go down, like Moses into Egypt, to lead them out." She spoke with a God who willed freedom and convinced her, according to her biographer, to be "ready to kill for freedom, if that was necessary, and defend the act as her religious right." During her rescue trips, she sang the spiritual "Go Down Moses" to announce her presence to plantation laborers. Slaves called her Moses.

Once free, African Americans were able to directly challenge the hypocrisy of Christian masters and proslavery doctrines. Anthony Burns, who escaped from slavery in Richmond in 1854 only to be recaptured, heard in prison he was excommunicated by his white Baptist congregation. His defended himself: "You charge me that in escaping, I disobeyed God's law. No indeed! That law which God wrote upon the table of my heart, inspiring the love of freedom, and impelling me to seek it at every hazard, I obeyed, and by the good hand of my God upon men, I walked out of the house of bondage." Finally freed, Burns became an ordained minister for fugitive slaves living in Canada.

Christianity inspired northern antislavery forces. In 1846, the Reverend Moses Dickson and eleven other African Americans formed the Knights of Tabor, dedicated "to strike the blow for liberty." They believed "God was with Israel, and gave the victory to the bondsmen, though they were opposed by twenty times their number. Our cause is just, and we believe in the justice of the God of Israel and the rights of man."

No less than Christianity, the lyrics of secular and spiritual music became a battleground that pitted master against slave. Though songs such as "Sometimes I Feel Like a Motherless Child" sounded a note of sad resignation, African-American music was usually upbeat, looking toward happier days and victo-

Harriet Tubman was inspired by her Christianity to liberate three
hundred slaves.

ries over old foes. In this music the devil, often a stand-in for the white exploiter, is more comic than powerful. And he can easily be fooled by a clever slave.

> *The Devil's mad and I'm glad,*
> *He lost the soul he thought he had.*

Planters and slaves fought a long tug of war for control of the slaves' music, its themes, words, and tempo. On her Georgia plantation, Fanny Kemble wrote that "many masters and overseers on these plantations prohibit melancholy tunes or words and encourage nothing but cheerful music." Some banned "any reference to particular hardships."

Masters demanded an accelerated beat in work songs in order to speed up labor in fields or on docks. A Richmond tobacco factory manager explained: "We encourage their singing as much as we can, for the boys work better while singing." When whites manipulated the musical tempo to increase production, African-American laborers tried to slow the beat to relieve the strain.

Planters also liked slaves to sing so they could check on their location and be sure they hadn't run off. "Make a noise, make a noise," overseers ordered slaves, reported Frederick Douglass. Singing by slaves acted like the bell around the cow's neck that always gave its exact location.

Slaves sang, but for their own reasons—to raise spirits, to affirm a sense of community, or to set a pace that would accomplish difficult jobs without injuries. When forced to sing, wrote Douglass, black voices often "told a tale of grief and sorrow. In the most boisterous outbursts of rapturous sentiment, there was ever a tinge of deep melancholy." Douglass "heard the same wailing notes" when he visited Ireland during the potato famine.

Slaves often used their music as a form of protest against evil people and conditions. In 1774, a white visitor, Nicolas Cresswell, wrote: "In their songs they generally relate the usage they have received from their Masters and Mistresses in a very satirical style and manner." Douglass remembered nonsense songs in which a sudden, "sharp hit was given to the meanness of slaveholders."

For people denied any political rights, including a right to speak up, lyrics in a song could deliver an incisive analysis or criticism. This short jingle offered humor, wit, and insight:

> *My ole Mistress promise me,*
> *When she died, she'd set me free,*
> *She lived so long dat her head got bald,*
> *An' she give out'n de notion of dyin' at all.*

To raise a hand against a white could mean death. To raise a laughing voice in a ditty involved no great risk:

> *Jackass rared*
> *Jackass pitched*
> *Throwed ol' massa in the ditch*

A clear understanding of slave exploitation was conveyed in a popular song about plantation production and distribution:

> *We raise the wheat,*
> *They give us the corn;*
> *We bake the bread*
> *They give us the crust;*
> *We sift the meal,*
> *They give us the skin,*
> *And that's the way*
> *They take us in.*

Sometimes songs spread important news. Some lyrics conveyed hidden messages to slaves that whites could not decipher. "Steal away, steal away, steal away to Jesus" encouraged runaways without warning masters. To tell blacks that one of their number had betrayed them, a song was used: "O Judyas he was a 'ceitful man, He went an' betray a most innocent man."

"Follow the Drinking Gourd" voiced love for freedom: "The old man is awaiting to carry you to freedom, so follow the drinking gourd." Another stanza detailed directions for runaways, telling them to follow the North Star to Canada.

During the Civil War the approach of the Union Army brought a new defiance to slave songs: "No more auction block for me, no more, no more." As Union soldiers drew closer, new lyrics were heard: "I want to cross over into campground" to that "promised land where all is peace."

In 1862, Susie King, twelve, and her grandmother stood in a Savannah church fervently singing an old hymn: "Yes, we all shall be free, When the Lord shall appear." The police rushed in and arrested all who were there, charging them with planning freedom and singing "the Lord" when they meant "Yankee."

Susie King smiled, for she knew freedom was rolling forth like an old spiritual, and neither police nor pattyrollers could stop the infectious music. Within months King was part of her people's liberation, a teacher of reading and writing for former slaves serving as soldiers in the Union Army. As an adult she wrote an autobiography of her exciting life.

Flight and Revolt

Runaways and Maroons

SEVEN

"I never saw the day since I knew anything that I didn't want to be free," remembered slave Anthony Bingey.

"Among the good trades I learned was the art of running away to perfection. I made a regular business of it," wrote Henry Bibb.

Beginning with the first arrivals from Africa, slaves fled their masters and overseers. Masters, said one, would "rather a negro do anything else than run away." Slaves left good masters and bad, easy work and hard. James Christian was not permitted to marry the woman of his choice. He fled a relaxed life in President John Tyler's White House.

✳Most runaways abandoned plantation work on the spur of the moment. These men and women were trying to escape a beating, prevent a sale to a new owner, or to search for nearby relatives and loved ones. Many ran to protest work, whippings, or evil overseers—and tried to remain hidden until they won promises of better conditions.

Others carefully planned to reach free land, and some tried to establish their own settlements in remote, hard-to-penetrate

A couple prepares to defend itself from slave-hunters.

swamps or mountains. From the New England Articles of Confederation in 1643 forward, European masters legally bound themselves to assist in the return of escaped slaves. Slaveholders had this pledge written into the U.S. Constitution and two federal Fugitive Slave acts. Slave-hunting was to be carried out by federal marshals and the U.S. Army if necessary.

Slaveholders would not tolerate any gap in their defense system. They bitterly resented Native American nations for accepting African Americans into their villages and were furious about an Indian adoption system that drew no color line. To seal off this escape hatch, Europeans demanded in treaties that Indian nations agree to return all fugitives. In 1721, the governor of Virginia had the Five Civilized Nations promise to surrender escapees, and in 1726, the governor of New York made the Iroquois Confederacy take the same pledge. In 1746, the Hurons promised, and the next year the Delawares promised. None returned a single fugitive. Many nations made clear they stood ready to fight for African men and women who had become their relatives and loved ones.

Along the Atlantic coast and spreading westward through woods and over mountains to the Mississippi, two dark races began to blend and marry. Artist George Catlin, writing in the 1830s, called the children of this mixture "the finest and most powerful men I have ever yet seen." From New England to the Carolinas, and westward to Minnesota, masters had to confront guerrilla forces born of these American alliances in the woods.

The strongest U.S. coalition of red and black people flowered in Florida around 1776. African runaways from plantations in Georgia became the peninsula's first settlers and were soon joined by Seminoles fleeing oppression by the Creek nation. The alliance was solidified when the Africans taught the newcomers methods of rice cultivation learned in Senegambia and Sierra Leone, Africa.

The two dark peoples developed a prosperous and peaceful farming and grazing economy. They also built a military alliance based on potent guerrilla strike forces. Masters in Georgia and the Carolinas saw these successful, armed black communities acting as a beacon to draw off their slaves. They feared armed uprisings that could destroy their slave system.

To crush the alliance, Florida was repeatedly invaded by U.S. slave-hunting posses and troops and was finally purchased by the

In Florida, armed resistance by free Africans, slave runaways, and Seminole Indians began around 1776. This European print shows an African leader of these combined forces.

United States in 1819. Florida's African Seminoles led in challenging the U.S. in pitched battles and guerrilla resistance.

Between 1816 and 1858, the black and red soldiers of the Seminole nation held the U.S. Army, Navy, and Marines at bay. The cost of these Florida wars for the United States was $40 million, with 1,500 servicemen dead. At times half of the U.S. Army was deployed against the Seminole military alliance.

Whether it was to join the resistance in Florida, flee to relatives, or reach freedom in the North or West, the decision to escape filled slave hearts with fear. Lewis Clarke recalled: "All the white part of mankind, that he has ever seen, are enemies to him and all his kindred. How can he venture where none but white faces shall greet him?" The mere thought of abandoning wives, husbands, children, and loved ones deterred many, delayed others, and filled the moment with pain. In 1850, a New York convention of fugitive slaves recalled the decision:

"So galling was our bondage, that to escape from it, we suffered the loss of all things, and braved every peril, and endured every hardship. Some of us left parents, some wives, some children. Some of us were wounded with guns and dogs, as we fled. Some of us secreted ourselves in the suffocating holds of ships. Nothing was so dreadful to us as slavery."

To compound their problems, blacks were denied a knowledge of geography and fed calculated lies. William Johnson of Virginia was told the Detroit River was three thousand miles wide. Sidney Allen, an engineer on his master's boat, was told that in Canada "nothin' but black-eyed peas could be raised." Susie King heard Yankees would hitch black people to carts instead of horses.

The entire white South was taught to be alert for fugitives, and masters were ready to dispatch armed posses. Regular patrols, the pattyrollers, were drafted for six cents an hour, a militia that nightly searched for fugitives in the woods and hills.

Some men ran a thriving business raising and training bloodhounds for these hunts. Dan McCowan advertised: "My hounds is well trained, and I have had 15 yeres experience. My rates is 10 dullers per hed of ketched in the beate where the master lives; 15 dullers in the county, and 50 dullers out of the county." One trained bloodhound cost $300, but it was worth it when the problem of fleeing slaves became an epidemic.

Tracking runaways was a dangerous and difficult job. "Some of 'em would rather be shot than be took," a white worker told reporter Olmsted. One deputy armed with a warrant followed his man into Virginia's Dismal Swamp only to find him standing neck deep in water. The deputy quietly returned to headquarters, erased the man's name from the warrant, and wrote "Seeable but not Comeatable."

Masters often advertised for runaway slaves in local newspapers. These descriptions by owners reveal some important truths about people—their skills, their abilities to read, write, and speak Indian or foreign languages, their determined efforts to reach loved ones.

Fugitives were described as bearing the scars of beatings, whippings, or brandings ("R" for those who ran before). It was clear what they were running from. Cut into the backs of men and women was the evidence of resistance. Sarah Grimke told of a teenage seamstress who ran away so often she was whipped until her back was lacerated. Then a "heavy iron collar, with three prongs projecting from it, was placed around her neck . . . to serve as a mark to describe her, in case of escape."

Owners described some runaways as "impudent and insolent," "notorious," or "unruly scoundrels." But others were called humble, cheerful, and loyal men and women who "had no reason to leave." In 1846, a Louisiana master wrote of three runaways: the first "very industrious" and "always answered with a smile"; the second "an industrious boy" who spoke to whites "very humbly, with his hand to his hat"; the third also addressed whites "humbly and respectfully with a smile."

A study of southern newspapers from 1732 to 1790 found that there were 7,846 fugitives advertised, and the vast majority were young men. But women, including those who were pregnant, carrying infants, or leading small children, numbered 10 percent in Maryland, 12 percent in Virginia and North Carolina, and more than 18 percent in Georgia and South Carolina. In South Carolina, for example, 3,746 runaways were men, 698 were women (including 14 who were pregnant), and 122 were children.

These notices described Africans who fled in the company of white indentured servants or received help from whites or free blacks. But most were on their own. In 1785, a South Carolina planter advertised for four generations of women—a grandmother, mother, and daughter "with a young child." In 1789, a Romeo and a Juliet fled together from slavery in Virginia. The next year four men and two women fled Georgia. One, Sue, was "lame with rheumatism," but managed to carry her three children, Juno, ten, Sarah seven, and Dolly, three.

Sometimes large numbers fled together. In 1779, the Edings plantation on Edisto Island, Georgia, lost thirty-six, including twelve women, who left together. Writing a year and a half after they left, Mr. Edings optimistically promised any "returning home of their own accord will be forgiven." In 1826, twenty-seven Kentucky slaves were being transported down the Ohio River by boat when they broke away. Swinging clubs, axes, and knives, they killed five whites, seized and sank the boat, and fled to Indiana. In 1830, a white complained that in four North Carolina counties slaves "come and go as they please, and if an attempt is made to stop them, they immediately fly to the woods . . . for months."

Mass flights to freedom were more common in the border states of Virginia, Kentucky, Tennessee, Maryland, and Delaware than the deep South. In 1826, a large number of runaways boarded a boat and sailed to the north during a Portsmouth, Virginia, celebration of the fiftieth anniversary of the Declaration of Independence. In 1845, some men and women from two Maryland counties armed themselves with clubs, swords, knives, a pistol, and a gun and began a march northward. They were captured.

In August 1848, Patrick Doyle, a white Danville, Ohio, college student, organized a band of seventy-five armed blacks in Kentucky heading toward the Ohio River. They fought two pitched battles with posses before being captured. Three black leaders were executed, and Doyle was sentenced to twenty years in jail.

Mass escapes were not uncommon. These twenty-eight people fled eastern Maryland.

These massive escapes could be classified as armed revolts.

Some individuals were fearless of punishments. They fled repeatedly or dared the impossible. A couple, Remus and Patty, fled a Battle, Alabama, plantation in 1836 only to be captured and jailed in Montgomery. They escaped to Georgia, were recaptured in Columbus, and again escaped, this time for good. In 1842, a slave named Abraham cleverly forged his own freedom papers in Mobile, Alabama, and reached Baltimore. When he was arrested, his imitation documents fooled a judge and he was released and reached the North.

Six men escaped from Key West, Florida, in 1858 in a small boat and sailed to the Bahamas. They decided to write their masters. Most wrote insulting letters, a few apologized for taking his good horse, and one signed his letter "Your most obedient servant." Sometimes fugitives sent masters bills for their labor.

Trouble stalked the road to freedom. Teenagers William and Charles Parker fled Maryland only to be confronted by three whites who knew they were fugitives. The black youths chased them off, but had to run as "every house was lighted up" and "we heard people talking and horses galloping this way and that way." The brothers finally reached safety in Pennsylvania.

Some trips took a long time. In Texas, a slave-hunter told of chasing a runaway for weeks: "We caught him once, but he got away . . . he gave me a kick in the face, and broke. I had my six-shooter handy, and I tried to shoot him, but every barrel missed fire. . . . We shot at him three times with rifles, but he'd got too far off. . . . We chased him and my dog got close to him once . . . but he had a dog himself, and . . . fit my dog." The black man reached Mexico, where slavery had been abolished in 1829.

In 1855, young Ann Wood led a Christmas eve flight of her friends from Virginia, but they were surrounded by an armed posse. Wood calmly raised her double-barreled pistol, waved a long knife, and told the whites to step aside or blood would flow that night. The posse galloped off, and Ann Wood and friends reached Philadelphia.

Ann Wood and her companions drive off slave-hunters.

At least two African Americans had friends ship them to freedom from southern cities. Henry Brown climbed into a box in Richmond, Virginia, and had a white friend mail him to the Philadelphia antislavery office. Sometimes he traveled upside down, but he survived to write a book and to become a national hero. William Peel Jones climbed into a box in Baltimore and spent seventeen hours in a steamboat before reaching Philadelphia.

Escape disguises and techniques ranged from clever to ingenious. Blacks pretended to be free or white, men became women, and women men. Some, dressed as sailors, took jobs on ships. Runaways threw off the scent of bloodhounds with pepper, dead fish, or by rubbing graveyard bones on their clothes. Some pretended to ask whites for directions, then headed along another road. Others escaped on rafts built from fence posts and across bridges built from sleds.

From Tennessee, Mr. and Mrs. John Little walked to Chicago.

Henry Brown is rescued from his box in Philadelphia.

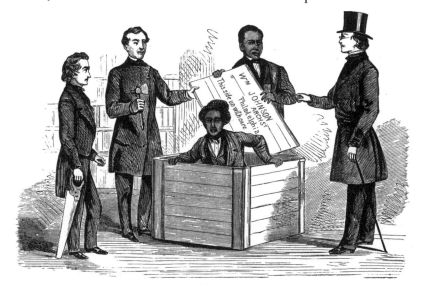

Maria Weems escaped slavery dressed as a man.

Mrs. Little, who was seventeen at the time, later remembered: "My shoes gave out before many days—then I wore my husband's old shoes till they were used up. Then we came barefoot all the way to Chicago. My feet were so blistered and sore and my ankles swollen, but I had to keep on. There was something driving me."

Fugitives sometimes built a new life for themselves in nearby woods or a far-off wilderness. A woman named Tamar lived in a forest and sometimes secretly hid under the floor of her mother's slave hut. "Her husband would sometimes spend part of the night with her and get back before sunrise. . . . We all supplied her," recalled a relative. Tamar had three children while living the life of an outlaw. Cornelia Carney recalled her father, who was beaten every time he ran away, decided to live in the woods with a cousin and another man. Saturday night or Sunday after whites left for church, he would return to his family.

Some runaways who could not reach Florida or the North began their own maroon colonies. They planted crops, hunted for game, and reared and educated families in parts of the Allegheny Mountains or Blue Ridge Mountains where posses had trouble penetrating. About two hundred people lived in the thirty-mile-long, fifteen-mile-wide Great Dismal Swamp, which stretches from Virginia into North Carolina. In 1842, a New Orleans paper reported three hundred runaways—"all armed"—lived in three nearby swamp areas.

Octave Johnson, twenty-one, had been raised as a cooper and treated well. He had seen his mother sold away when he was a teenager. Threatened by an overseer, Johnson fled from New Orleans to live as a maroon for a year and a half. His tale of maroon life, dictated to a U.S. Army officer in 1864, reveals the kind of daring cooperation between men and women it took to survive behind an armed enemy: "I had to steal my food; took turkeys, chickens, and pigs; before I left, our number had increased to thirty, of whom ten were women; we were four miles in the rear of the plantation house; sometimes we would rope the beef cattle and drag them to our hiding place; we obtained matches from our friends on the plantation; we slept on logs and burned cypress leaves to make a smoke and keep away mosquitoes; Eugene Jardeau, master of hounds, hunted for us for three months; often those at work would betray those in the swamp, for fear of being implicated in their escape; we furnished meat to our fellow-servants in the field, who would return corn meal; one day twenty hounds came after me; I called the party to my assistance and we killed eight of the bloodhounds."

One of history's most complicated and daring escapes was planned by William and Ellen Craft in Georgia. In 1848, the Crafts decided to leave because they wanted to have a baby in freedom. Ellen, almost white in complexion, cut her hair short and dressed in the clothing of her owner. Claiming she had a toothache, she wrapped her beardless face in a shawl. William was "his" servant.

They took enough money to travel by railroad and steamer and stayed at the best hotels. Since Ellen could not write, she carried her right arm in sling so she had an excuse not to sign hotel registers. Dark glasses, a slight limp, a cane, and a pretense of partial deafness helped Ellen avoid conversations that could give her away. She was a sick young man, journeying north for medical treatment and in true aristocratic style, attended by her black servant. Despite all her careful preparations, several times she barely avoided exposure.

In Philadelphia, the Vigilance Committee provided guards and spirited the couple to Boston. In an African-American boardinghouse the Crafts had a legal marriage performed by abolitionist minister Theodore Parker. He concluded the ceremony by handing the groom a sword "to save his wife's liberty." The couple left to build their family in the safety of England.

For the Crafts and most others, flight was an act of reckless daring, yet an estimated thirty thousand escaped in the decades before the Civil War. Fugitives had to depend almost entirely on their own wits. Robert Purvis, a black abolitionist who assisted those who reached Philadelphia, reported, "Many of the fugitives required no other help than advice and direction how to proceed."

White antislavery people helped, but African-American communities in the South proved crucial. Purvis recalled: "The most efficient helpers or agents we had were two market-women, who lived in Baltimore."

"Ham and Eggs," the code name for a black agent in Petersburg, Virginia, wrote to William Still, underground railroad leader in Philadelphia: "I want you to know that I feel as much determined to work in the glorious cause, as ever I did in the all of my life, and I have some very good hams on hand that I would like very much for you to have."

Eliza Baines of Portsmouth, Virginia, placed runaways on ships to Boston and New Bedford.

Fugitive slaves living in the North formed secret networks to

William Still, head of the Philadelphia station and author of *The Underground Railroad.*

aid those in flight. In Cairo, Illinois, George Burroughes, a black porter on the Illinois Central railroad to Chicago, aided all he could. William Wells Brown ran a Lake Erie steamboat that carried runaways from Detroit or Buffalo. He wrote: "In the year 1842, I conveyed from the first of May to the first of December, 69 fugitives over Lake Erie to Canada."

John H. Hooper, a Maryland escapee, ran the underground railroad station in Troy, New York. Frederick Douglass ran one in Rochester, New York. Louis Washington, a Richmond runaway, ran a station in Columbus, Ohio.

From Canada, white reformer Samuel Gridley Howe reported that, in the ten years before the Civil War, five hundred ex-slaves, "not content with personal freedom and happiness, went secretly back to their old homes, and brought away their wives and children at much peril and cost." Harriet Beecher Stowe modeled her gentle "Uncle Tom" after Josiah Henson, but the real Henson was a daring man who brought out 118 people from bondage.

Runaways who reached the North were often pursued by posses who seized and returned them. The 1793 Fugitive Slave Act imposed a $500 fine on any person who harbored or aided an escapee. But in the first fugitive case in Boston, the prisoner bolted for freedom. While in court, the captured man knocked down two policemen and raced through the crowd.

In New York City, in 1801, 1826, and 1828, African Americans rioted against "blackbirds" or slave catchers from the South coming to capture runaways. By the late 1830s, a Committee of Vigilance battled "blackbirds" in the streets and courtrooms.

African-American communities in the North and their white friends increasingly defied the law to provide armed assistance to fugitives. Boston minister Theodore Parker announced, "The first business of the anti-slavery men is to help the fugitives; we, like Christ, are to seek and save that which is lost."

Perhaps the most determined flight from bondage was by a man who could not run. "General" was a tailor who fled the Virginia of Patrick Henry and Thomas Jefferson. In November 1784, his owner, Landon Carter, wrote a reward notice that described "General" as "very remarkable as a runaway having lost both his legs, cut off near the knees."

The bravest figure in the effort to rescue slaves was probably Harriet Tubman. At fifteen, as she helped a man trying to escape, her head caught the force of a two-pound weight thrown by an overseer. From then on, dizzy spells and sleeping seizures came on her without warning. She married John Tubman, but when he refused to join her escape from eastern Maryland in 1848, she left with her two brothers. When they lost heart and returned, she reached freedom alone.

Tubman found a calling to help others and for the next ten years returned nineteen times to Atlantic seaboard slave states. She aided three hundred men, women, and children—loved ones and perfect strangers—to escape. She carried a pistol for enemies and the faint of heart, and potions to quiet crying infants. She proudly claimed, "I never lost a single passenger."

A reward of $40,000 was offered for her dead or alive, but she never stopped. She stated her simple creed: "There was one of two things I had a right to, liberty, or death; if I could not have one, I would have the other; for no man should take me alive; I should fight for my liberty as long as my strength lasted."

Those who left the South were fleeing slavery, but they were running to a future as well. Henry Bibb became a noted antislavery lecturer. He campaigned for the Liberty Party in the U.S. and later settled in Canada, where he published that country's first black newspaper.

Henry Bibb relied on deception, as did most slaves, to fool their masters.

Lewis and Milton Clarke became abolitionist lecturers and authors, as did Frederick Douglass, William Wells Brown, and William and Ellen Craft.

The Parker brothers, who had their resistance training during their flight, armed and trained dozens of young African Americans in Pennsylvania. In 1851, the Parkers' volunteer army fired the first shots of the war against slavery (see Chapter 10).

During the Civil War, Octave Johnson left his maroon friends in Louisiana to become a corporal in a U.S. Army regiment. During the war Susie King served as a nurse and teacher for black soldiers. Harriet Tubman served as a U.S. Army scout behind Confederate lines in the Carolinas. She spent the rest of her life (she died in 1913) not living quietly, but running a retirement home for elderly former slaves.

Revolts in the Age of Revolution

EIGHT

Centuries before the minutemen bravely stood at Concord Bridge, African slave rebels struck for freedom. They introduced the idea of revolution to the British colonies long before white men wrote an eloquent Declaration of Independence. From the beginning, slave rebelliousness was a hallmark of life in colonial North America. "We are determined to shake off our bondage, and for that purpose we stand on a good foundation. Many have joined," said a black Charleston rebel.

Africans had been wrenched from societies that cherished liberty, practiced justice, and treasured the young and the elderly. Though untrained, unarmed, and vastly outnumbered by the armed society around them, they repeatedly attempted insurrection.

In the earliest slave rebellions blacks often united with Indians. In 1526, the two races joined in a North Carolina coastal revolt that sent the surviving European colonists packing for home. When Native Americans besieged Jamestown in 1622, whites died, but Africans were spared. In 1657, Africans and Indians invaded Hartford, Connecticut. In 1727, the two peoples threatened Virginia settlements. During Pontiac's uprising in 1763, a white Detroit resident complained, "The Indians are saving and caressing all the Negroes they take."

To prevent solidification of a force that could spell their doom, British officials heated up ancient rivalries and ignited new ones. In 1758, South Carolina governor James Glenn proclaimed, "It has always been the policy of this government to create an aversion in them [Indians] to Negroes."

Divide and rule became British colonial policy. Africans were armed to fight Indians and Indians bribed to hunt runaways. For recapturing runaways, Indians received thirty-five deerskins in Virginia, and three blankets and a musket in the Carolinas. Local Indian nations often refused to hunt people they had befriended, so Europeans recruited other nations living at a distance.

The eighteenth century, which ended with the American and French revolutions, first gave birth to slave uprisings from New York to Georgia. In 1712, New York slaves rose to kill and wound more than a dozen whites. Then rebellions flared in Virginia and the Carolinas.

Soon fearful South Carolina whites, outnumbered by their slaves, armed when leaving for church. In 1739, three uprisings rocked the colony. The largest was at Stono River, where rebels seized a warehouse full of guns and ammunition. An eyewitness described their advance: "Being thus provided with arms, they elected one of their number captain, and agreed to follow him, marching toward the southwest, with colours flying and drums beating, like a disciplined company." About thirty whites died. Troops surrounded and massacred the African-American rebels.

New York City, in 1740, faced another insurrection, and the following year another one. In 1741, authorities executed thirty-one African rebels and four whites who helped them. In Georgia, in 1770, where slavery had been installed only a generation before, there was a major insurrection. In 1775, as tension between English rulers and colonists mounted, a slave outbreak shook North Carolina.

These rebellious slaves prepared the colonists to challenge British tyranny. Before they rose against King George III, often white American patriots were trained in slave-fighting armies—battling against people striking for liberty.

In reaching for arguments to justify their thirst for independence from England, the Founding Fathers claimed "all men are created equal" and have a right to freedom. They justified revolution against unjust or tyrannical authority. Some carried the issue of liberty further. James Otis, Benjamin Franklin, and Tom Paine denounced slavery. In 1774, Abigail Adams, writing to her famous husband, John, about a slave plot, said, "It always appeared a most iniquitous scheme to me to fight ourselves for what we are daily robbing and plundering from those who have as good a right to freedom as we have."

In his first draft of the Declaration of Independence, Jefferson denounced King George III for promoting the African slave trade. But Jefferson's criticism was eliminated after pressure from slaveholding delegates to the Continental Congress. As American revolutionists marched forth against British rule, northern colonies abandoned slavery. Some patriots, such as Benjamin Franklin and Alexander Hamilton, began antislavery societies because ending bondage seemed a normal step in building a republican society.

But the white South, with hundreds of thousands of slaves, increased nightly patrols. South Carolina announced a bounty of a healthy slave for any white who enlisted as a soldier in the Continental Army or Navy.

The American "right of revolution" fired black imaginations as much as it did white. In 1765, the Sons of Liberty paraded in Charleston chanting, "Liberty." A few months later African

Americans took to the same streets shouting for independence. Whites rushed for their muskets, remained under arms for a week, and sent out patrols day and night. In Virginia, in 1767, slaves were executed for poisoning overseers. In 1774, African Americans rose in Georgia and killed seven whites.

The month before minutemen faced British muskets at Lexington and Concord, slaves in Ulster County, New York, organized an uprising that also involved five hundred Indians By summer 1775, patriots found armed slaves a menace from Maryland to Georgia. Hundreds, perhaps thousands, struck in three North Carolina counties but were crushed by overwhelming white firepower.

On July 4, 1776, John Hancock's bold scrawl reached across the Declaration of Independence. The next day, a letter from Somerset, New Jersey, informed him slaves were "arming and attempting to form themselves" for their liberty. In the first two years of the American Revolution, slave unrest erupted behind patriot lines from New York to Louisiana.

The British tried to seize on slave unrest to draw off black laborers and arm them against the patriots. On November 7, 1775, Royal Governor Lord Dunsmore's proclamation offered liberty and a musket to any slave who fled to his lines. "The flame runs like wildfire through the slaves," a white woman wrote in early December. Soon thousands of African Americans crowded into British camps. Thomas Jefferson estimated 30,000 escaped in 1778. In the revolution about 100,000 slaves fled their masters.

By January 1776, General Washington, who had refused black volunteers, reversed his policy. Some 5,000 African Americans, slaves and free blacks, served in the Continental army and navy. Their service was generally much longer than white volunteers, and their record of bravery earned battlefield commendations and awards of freedom.

Most African Americans fought in integrated units, and a few northern states, such as Rhode Island, fielded all-black regiments (under white officers). Like the blacks who wore British redcoats, what these patriots sought was liberty. Many African-American veterans on both sides found it.

This first war against colonialism and for liberty inspired people the world over and none more passionately than African Americans. Beginning in 1773, blacks, particularly in Massachusetts, adopted the Revolution's slogans to agitate for their liberty. One black petition reminded officials that Africans "are a freeborn Pepel and have never forfeited this Blessing" and have "in common with all other men a natural right to our freedoms." Another cited the Declaration of Independence's "unalienable right" to liberty. In 1780, African-American petitions protested against "taxation without representation."

Americans hoped their victory would trigger waves of democratic revolution, topple kings, and establish just governments in the world. Wrote Thomas Jefferson, "We are pointing out the way to struggling nations who wish, like us, to emerge from their tyrannies also." Friends of republicanism cheered when the people of Paris liberated the Bastille prison, executed their king, and began to build their own democratic government.

Even as the French wrote their Declaration of the Rights of Man, the new democratic spirit spawned a revolution across the Atlantic in one of France's Caribbean colonies. San Domingo's sugar made it the richest colony in the world. France ruled this island of half a million enslaved Africans, four-fifths of the population, who labored under brutal masters and backbreaking conditions. (Today this island is called Hispaniola, and it contains the nations of Haiti and Santo Domingo.)

Almost half of the colony's free people were a mixture of white and black and were denied citizenship rights by the French. The French king's divide-and-rule policy kept the mixed population from siding with the slaves, but France's democratic revolution stirred both classes. First the mixed population revolted against French discrimination, then the slaves.

In 1791, massive slave revolts in San Domingo transformed the struggle among free people over their rights into a black revolution to overthrow slavery. By the next year slavery had ended. Toussaint L'Ouverture, fifty, a short, brilliant, slave coachman, became the revolution's charismatic military and political figure. He kept his island loyal to France and made strategic alliances with foreign powers. His armies drove armed Spanish and British invasions into the sea.

L'Ouverture never wavered in his pledge to end bondage. In 1797, he told the Directory, the five men who ruled France, of his people's determination—"We have known how to face dangers to obtain our liberty, we shall know how to brave death to maintain it." The United States traded with L'Ouverture but did not recognize his government.

Revolt in San Domingo.

When some slaveholders demanded his overthrow, a Pennsylvania legislator reminded his fellow citizens of a U.S. "insurrection" that secured "independence." For antislavery Americans, the successful revolt in San Domingo was seen as proof that U.S. slavery was doomed.

The rebellion bloodied the country as every side carried out fearful atrocities. In the United States, some whites warned that black suffering under bondage could also lead to widespread bloodshed. Slaveholders, on the other hand, blamed San Domingo's African rebels for the continuing violence. It proved, they insisted, blacks needed European masters with a whip hand.

Revenge taken by the black army for the cruelties practiced on them by the French.

When Napoleon seized power in France, L'Ouverture sent him a dispatch that included his 1801 constitution, which ended slavery and abolished government racial discrimination. An infuriated Napoleon wrote that the constitution rejected "the dignity and sovereignty" of France in favor of independence.

"Why should this not be so?" answered L'Ouverture. "The United States did exactly that; and with the assistance of monarchical France, succeeded." The black ruler rejected Napoleon's threats and bribes and the "hope you entertain that I might be induced to betray the cause."

Fresh from dazzling military victories in Italy, Napoleon decided to restore French power and slavery in San Domingo. He dispatched huge armies under the command of his brother-in-law, Leclerc. Though the French failed to defeat the revolution, Leclerc tricked L'Ouverture into a meeting aboard a French ship and seized him as a prisoner.

L'Ouverture stood on the deck and predicted, "In overthrowing me, you have cut down in San Domingo only the trunk of the tree of liberty. It will spring up again by the roots for they are numerous and deep."

Though L'Ouverture died in a cell in the Alps, his assistants, Jean-Jacques Dessalines and Henri Christophe, fought on. Christophe had served in the American Revolution and been wounded in the battle of Savannah in 1779. He was one of more than seven hundred blacks the French had recruited when they had helped the U.S. patriots.

Dessalines and Christophe continued the war until the French surrendered in November 1803. On New Year's Day, 1804, on the very spot L'Ouverture was captured by the French, a declaration of independence for the new republic of Haiti was announced. This proud Indian name identified the second republic of the New World. For the first and only time in history, slaves had liberated an entire country.

Ex-slaves and free blacks united in San Domingo to defeat armies from Spain, England, and France.

Napoleon's armies were soon defeated in Europe, but Haiti was the first to explode his global ambitions. Napoleon had hoped to build an empire in the New World by dispatching huge armies from bases in San Domingo and the Louisiana Territory. The slave rebels of Haiti changed his plans. Their revolt taught him how difficult it was to hold colonies across the Atlantic Ocean.

When U.S. diplomats arrived to purchase New Orleans from France, Napoleon made a new suggestion. For four cents an acre, he sold the entire Louisiana Territory to the United States.

The successful rebellion in San Domingo reached into U.S. homes. At first, it was celebrated as another victory for American revolutionary principles. But slaveholders soon convinced many whites it posed a threat to American security. The triumph of democracy was fine, they said, but only for people with fair complexions and European culture and manners. Some masters claimed their slaves became more menacing as news of Haiti spread to southern plantations.

Slaveholders feared their laborers would be contaminated by seeds of revolution from the West Indies. Thomas Jefferson was convinced that sparks from Haiti had the power to set the south-land afire. In 1782, southern states began to ban black refugees from Caribbean islands. South Carolina denied entrance to blacks from the West Indies, South America, or any French-ruled island. In 1803, the U.S. House of Representatives voted unanimously that refugees from San Domingo posed a "danger to the peace and safety of the United States."

A victorious, independent Haiti confirmed the worst fears of U.S. slaveholders. If armed slaves had defeated mighty Napoleon's armies in battle, what might be *their* fate? Until U.S. slavery ended, worried southern whites kept asking this question.

A growing number of whites who opposed slavery hoped Haiti would serve as an example to U.S. slaveholders. African Americans in Haiti, though they had been kept in ignorance, had been capable of defeating their owners. They saw and avenged their wrongs, learned and asserted their rights, and finally took power from foreigners to rule their own destiny. Some whites used this lesson of San Domingo to urge their countrymen to abolish slavery before it was too late.

But others insisted that only an overwhelming black majority produced success in Haiti. San Domingo had an 80 percent slave population towering over a small, bitterly divided free population. In addition, the European colonial powers in the region were at war. (In British Guiana and Jamaica, where slave insurrections also achieved success, blacks outnumbered whites by nine to one.)

These conditions did not exist in the southern states of the U.S., where African Americans formed a bare majority in only Mississippi and South Carolina (55 percent to 57 percent). These figures fell to 47 percent in Louisiana, 45 percent in Alabama, 44 percent in Georgia, 31 percent in Virginia, 25 percent in Tennessee, and only 20 percent in Kentucky. Unarmed people needed overwhelming numbers to defeat trained armies.

In the decades after the American Revolution, the U.S. ruling class accepted the slaveholders' command that the new national government must defend their human property. It was written into the new Constitution and laws of the land. At home, masters who loved their own freedom strengthened the vast control machinery that prevented slaves from achieving liberty. As people settled on the frontier, the remote, inaccessible havens where rebel armies could organize began to vanish. Revolts were much harder to launch and freedom more difficult to reach.

The African-American community drew its own conclusions from San Domingo's success. Haiti taught that thrusts for freedom did not always end in military defeat and painful death. Slave resistance had become global. L'Ouverture, Dessalines, and Christophe became inspiring role models. In slave cabins, at night, parents told children warming tales of a land not far away in the Americas where black freedom-fighters defeated powerful European tyrants and lived to rule the day.

Nineteenth-Century Slave Rebels

NINE

The American, French, and Haitian revolutions delivered messages about freedom that neither slaves nor masters could ignore. But as nineteenth-century slaves took heart and drew strength from victories over European rulers and bondage, U.S. slaveholders tightened control over their slaves.

One white southern response was to close off blacks from all information about resistance. Beginning with the American Revolution, and perhaps before, news of uprisings rarely appeared in print. In 1774, James Madison wrote of one revolt, "It is prudent that such attempts should be concealed as well as suppressed." In 1800, Virginia governor James Monroe asked the legislature to bury news about that year's massive conspiracy that threatened Richmond. He "hoped it would even pass unnoticed."

In 1808, Governor John Tyler advised against discussing revolts even at a closed session of the Virginia legislature. He feared it would "probably increase the spirit of insurrection among the slaves." Governor Tyler was admitting that slaves could penetrate a secret session of the state legislature.

Even traditional salutes to U.S. independence, some feared, became ammunition for slave rebels. "The celebration of the Fourth of July belongs exclusively to the white population," wrote a white Charlestonian. Keep blacks from Independence Day ceremonies lest they "imbibe false notions."

But the spirit of Toussaint L'Ouverture lived on in the slave quarters. In 1800, a U.S. *Gazette* reporter in Virginia wrote whites momentarily expected "a rising among the negroes . . . God only knows our fate." In 1822, a Charleston woman wrote a friend: "Last evening twenty-five hundred of our citizens were under arms to guard our property and lives. But it is a subject not to be mentioned; and unless you hear of it elsewhere, say nothing about it." These described two carefully directed plans by slaves to capture southern cities: Richmond in 1800 and Charleston in 1822.

While visiting the South, British reporter William H. Russell read "several dreadful accounts of murder and violence," where slaves rose against their owners. After interviewing planters and their wives, Russell concluded, "There is something suspicious in the constant never-ending statement that 'we are not afraid of our slaves.' " Though owners like to boast, "Our servants are perfectly happy," privately many admitted, "We are living on a volcano."

Whites knew what their reactions would be if white families were forced into slavery. Thoughts of bloody black retribution were never far from their minds. Panicky imaginations heard impending bloodshed in chance remarks, silly rumors, minor brawls, mysterious fires, and unsolved deaths.

Almost any challenge to white authority, even by a few, could be seen as a burning fuse leading to the slave quarter. Investigations ruled by the terror-stricken sent whites running for their guns, whips, and horses. Savage bloodletting was the easiest response to actual threats and imagined ones. Many times in the nineteenth century slaves tried to slash their way to freedom. But the lives they took never matched the barbarity and massive murders of the white reprisals that followed in their wake.

Separating black uprisings from white hysteria was difficult in the early nineteenth century and poses problems today. Since rebellion was "a subject not to be mentioned," evidence was buried. No black rebel survived to publish his or her story; most died quickly at the hands of state authorities or posses in the field. Rebel "confessions" were extracted by white officials and provide an incomplete picture of events. Much of what happened in each plot remains unclear—except there were numerous rebellions, many more conspiracies, and they were invariably crushed with unstinting brutality.

By the nineteenth century, slaveholder power rested on thousands of well-trained troops and command of communication and transportation. Slaves began with a few weapons, no military training, and perhaps a hope of seizing an enemy arsenal. They had no experience with guns, no way to practice being an army, and few places to hide once the militia appeared. Slave Solomon Northup wrote: "Without arms or ammunition, or even with them, I saw such a step would result in certain defeat, disaster, and death and always raised my voice against it."

Rebels had few good choices. If they involved too few, they could quickly be isolated and overwhelmed. If a leader expanded his conspiracy to hundreds or thousands, he risked betrayal by its weakest links. Many schemes were revealed by informers whom whites richly rewarded for their cooperation.

To avoid inevitable exposure, some leaders planned surprise attacks that would seize weapons and recruit volunteers on the way. This idea rested on a shaky faith. Slaves on the rebels' line of march would be asked to risk their lives for those they hardly knew, who suddenly appeared with a plan nobody had time to explain fully. Even if some joined the ranks, could this spontaneous, unarmed rabble stand up against the trained military units whites were bound to summon?

Despite the dangers, time and again those in chains attempted insurrection. Their decision often came as a last desperate stab for freedom and at a system that held their lives and families in contempt.

Four major slave rebellions shook the South during the first half of the nineteenth century. For African-American communities the leaders became legends in the tradition of Toussaint L'Ouverture and Henri Christophe. Whites shuddered at the names.

In 1800, in Henrico County, Virginia, Gabriel Prosser, twenty-four, six foot two, with no record of resistance, plotted for months to capture Richmond. A blacksmith taught to read by his master's wife, Prosser was a devoted student of the Old Testament. Samson was his hero. With his wife, Nanny, and his brothers, Solomon and Martin, on the night of August 30, 1800, Prosser assembled on his master's estate a force estimated at more than nine hundred.

Some carried scythes and clubs, others bayonets, and a few had guns. Prosser and his officers, knowing of L'Ouverture's alliance with France, planned to spare Frenchmen and Quakers, and to recruit Catawba Indians and poor whites. His strategy was to divide his forces into three columns under previously selected officers, capture Richmond's armory, and subdue the city. Believing fifty thousand blacks and "friends of humanity" would join him, he foresaw a victory as great as the one in Haiti.

A sudden storm brought floods that poured over the six miles of roads to Richmond. The conspirators were drenched, isolated from their target, and disheartened. Convinced heaven had spoken, they went home to wait for a better omen.

The conspiracy began to unravel. Prosser and his officers were betrayed, captured, and sentenced to death. One bravely told his captors he had done for African Americans what Washington had done for Americans: "I have ventured my life . . . to obtain the liberty of my countrymen."

Though federal intervention was unneeded, Governor James

Monroe requested and received permission to use the Federal Armory at Manchester. Thus, a federal government made its first commitment to crush slave revolts. The governor's investigation claimed the Prosser plot "embraced most of the slaves" in and near the city and "perhaps the whole state."

Governor Monroe had served in the Revolutionary Army and studied law with Thomas Jefferson. Now this former revolutionary came to interview the present one. The governor left no record of the exchange. Prosser "seems to have made up his mind to die" in silence, he wrote. Monroe later added, "Unhappily, while this class of people exists among us, we can never count with certainty on its tranquil submission."

Gabriel Prosser and thirty to forty followers were hanged at the Richmond jail, but even as they died, some whites spoke of their "true spirit of heroism" and "utmost composure." This led to an open debate in Virginia on continuing slavery. Slaveholder John Randolph said, "The accused have exhibited a spirit, which, if it becomes general, must deluge the Southern country in blood. They manifested a sense of their rights and a contempt of danger and a thirst for revenge which portend the most unhappy consequences."

Governor Monroe believed the danger to the public posed by slave unrest "is daily increasing." He corresponded with his friend, President Thomas Jefferson, about placing free black people on frontier land. In a series of secret sessions, the Virginia legislature debated ending slavery, but put off a decision.

Grave warnings came from other southerners. George Tucker wrote a popular pamphlet stating that "the love of freedom is an inborn sentiment" given by God to all humans from philosophers to slaves. "At the first favorable moment, it springs forth, and flourishes with a vigor that defies all check." Tucker wanted to free all slaves, but whites would not sacrifice so rich a treasure.

The controversy provoked by Prosser's revolt reached beyond

Virginia. Mississippi governor Winthrop Sergeant warned his people to expect uprisings. By 1802, northern states (except New Jersey) had ended bondage. Maryland, Tennessee, and Kentucky soon made manumission, or the granting of liberty to slaves, easier. Legislatures in Maryland and Kentucky discussed gradual emancipation, but no southern state seriously considered abolishing slavery.

In June 1802, a Norfolk paper published a slave woman's letter (with her original spelling): "White pepil be-ware of your lives, their is a plan now forming and intended to be put in execution this harvest time. They are to commence and use their sithes as weapons until they can get possession of other weapons; there is a great many weapons hid for the purpose, and be you assured if you do not look out in time that many of you will be put to death." By October, twenty African-American rebels were in jail.

In 1808, the U.S. Congress, fearful of violence from newly enslaved Africans, banned the slave trade.

A new round of slave outbreaks came during the conflict between the United States and England that became the War of 1812. In January 1811, an African American who signed himself as "J.B." wrote a letter to "General T.R." that was discovered in Richmond. It confirmed white fears. "J.B." wrote of eighty armed rebels and urged secrecy "till that fateful night."

In St. John the Baptist Parish, thirty-six miles from New Orleans, that same year, what was probably the largest U.S. slave rebellion erupted. Some five hundred blacks marched toward the city from the Andry estate. They destroyed five plantations and picked up recruits along the way. Orderly companies under officers carried flags, and men walked to the beat of drums. Louisiana's governor summoned federal troops. General Wade Hampton's six hundred militiamen surrounded the rebels, executed sixty-eight, and ended the revolution.

During the war of 1812, slaves fled to whomever promised

freedom. A U.S. officer reported: "Our negroes are flocking to the enemy from all quarters, whom they convert into troops, vindictive and rapacious—with the most minute knowledge of every by-path, they return upon us as guides." John Randolph urged his fellow Virginians to worry less about British troops and more about "our safety at home."

In 1816, George Boxley, a white Virginia store owner popular among African Americans, led a slave revolt. Believing "the distinction between rich and poor was too great," he recruited white assistants in Fredericksburg and Richmond. When his plan was betrayed, Boxley managed to escape, but six black rebels were executed.

In 1822, Denmark Vesey, a Charleston carpenter, conspired to seize the city. Vesey was a slave until he won a lottery in 1800 and used the winnings to purchase his freedom. He found, though, he was not allowed to buy his family's freedom. A leading member of the Hamstead African Methodist church, Vesey had also traveled widely in the Caribbean and read everything he could find about slavery and Haiti. L'Ouverture's success and the biblical tale of the Hebrews' rescue excited Vesey and his co-plotters.

In 1821, when whites closed his Hamstead church, Vesey felt it was "high time for us to seek for our rights." "If we are only unanimous and courageous, as the San Domingo people were," Vesey said, "we were fully able to conquer the whites."

Vesey calculated that a bold strike in Charleston would send eager blacks from nearby plantations rushing to him. Slave masters would flee and their empire would collapse. The plotters discussed fleeing to Africa or the Caribbean if their plan failed, but specific transportation was not arranged.

By May, Vesey recruited an estimated six to nine thousand. Now the plot became vulnerable to informers, and by early June whites had penetrated it. On June 22, Vesey and other leaders were arrested by state authorities. Governor Thomas Bennett quickly requested federal aid. Secretary of War Calhoun, a South Carolina slaveholder, dispatched federal artillery troops from St. Augustine to South Carolina. He did not inform the president, though only the president of the United States has the constitutional power to send federal troops into states.

Conspirators were dealt with quickly. Of Vesey's band, thirty-five were hanged, forty-two exiled, and four whites were convicted of aiding the conspiracy. On the gallows the doomed shouted out to keep revolt alive. Federal troops stood by to quell any rescue effort by the African-American community.

The last major slave revolt, organized by Nat Turner in 1831, shook the foundations of slavery in Southampton, Virginia, and throughout the South. Turner, at thirty, was a slave whom whites

Some 250 slave plots and rebellions marked the years of bondage in North America. This old print shows Nat Turner and his men.

had always considered a quiet, contented man. Then one night he had a vision that his duty was to end bondage. Deeply religious and a country lay preacher on Sundays, Turner was respected far and wide for his piety and leadership.

Turner set about his new task, picking early morning as the time of revolution. On August 22, with sixty to eighty men, most on horseback, Turner led his forces toward the county seat of Jerusalem and its store of arms and ammunition. In the next forty hours, Turner and his men spared a poor white family, but slew fifty-seven to sixty-five white masters and their families.

Federal troops from Fort Monroe, the Navy ships *Warren* and *Natchez* near Norfolk, and the *Hampton* with three artillery companies were rushed to Southampton. U.S. Marine guards and sailors from the *Warren* and *Natchez* marched through the county to announce a federal presence and terrify any African Americans thinking of joining Turner's rebellion.

A vast roundup began, but Turner escaped capture by hiding in the woods. He finally walked out and surrendered. Sentenced to death, Nat Turner reminded his captors that Christ had been crucified and calmly went to the gallows.

The revolt's slayings were soon surpassed by those of white vigilantes. With torch and rifle, fanatical men swooped down on black communities throughout the countryside. An estimated two hundred men, women, and children were slain, most with no connection to the rebellion. Reprisals reached counties besides Southampton and states beyond Virginia. "The best and the brightest was killed in Nat's time," recalled Charity Bowery, a slave in Edenton, North Carolina.

African Americans celebrated "Ole Prophet Nat" by singing, "You can't keep the world from turnin' 'round / Or Nat Turner from gainin' ground." For whites, Turner was their worst nightmare in flesh and blood. One slaveholder admitted, "I have not slept without anxiety in three months. Our nights are sometimes spent in listening to noises." Nat Turner died on the gallows, but

His revolt crushed, Nat Turner hid in Southampton County until October 30, 1831, when he surrendered to Benjamin Phipps.

his ghostly spirit hovered above every southerner.

Slaveholder James McDowell told the Virginia legislature the uprising raised the "suspicion that a Nat Turner might be in every family, that the same bloody deeds might be acted over at any time in any place, that the material for it was spread throughout the land, and always ready for a like explosion."

Mrs. Lawrence Lewis, niece of George Washington, wrote about "a smothered volcano—we know not when or where the flame will burst forth, but we know that death in the most horrid forms threatens us. Some have died, others have become deranged."

Southern legislatures voted their fears. Since Turner read and preached, laws were passed against black preachers and banning the teaching of slaves. "To see you with a book in your hand, they would almost cut your throat," recalled one slave. Laws were passed in many southern states that made manumission of slaves almost impossible.

One Virginia legislator spoke of his goal for slaves: "We have, as far as possible, closed every avenue by which light might enter their minds. If you could extinguish the capacity to see the light, our work would be completed; they would then be on a level with the beasts of the field, and we should be safe!"

The massacres carried out in the wake of Turner's revolt were designed to terrorize black communities. However, two mutinies on the slave-trading ships showed even terror had its limitations. In 1839, Joseph Cinqué, son of an African king, led fifty-four Africans being transported to the New World in a revolt aboard the *Amistad*. The Africans tried to steer back to their homeland, but treacherous white crewmen guided the ship toward the Connecticut coast. Interned at first, Cinqué and his men were finally

Joseph Cinqué lead fifty-four Africans in a mutiny aboard the *Amistad*.

The slave rebellion on the *Amistad* led to freedom for the Africans.

freed by the U.S. Supreme Court. Former president John Quincy Adams served as their volunteer lawyer.

In 1841, Madison Washington led a mutiny of 19 on the *Creole* sailing from Hampton Roads, Virginia, with a cargo of 135 slaves for New Orleans. Washington and his people sailed to the Bahamas. They were warmly welcomed there by fellow Africans who sailed out in small boats to surround a liberated *Creole*.

The end of the eighteenth century had brought models of successful revolutions against tyranny to the Americas. But it also brought profound changes to slave communities. They were no longer dominated by people who had lived or been fighters in Africa, or who were steeped in its cultures. Slaves remained powerless, uneducated, and unarmed in the nineteenth century, while U.S. industrial might and military power soared. Slaveholder surveillance over, and brutality toward, slaves rose.

Pioneer families settled in the hills and back country that might once have been home to maroon colonies. New roads were built and trains reached into frontier regions. These opened a continent to whites and closed it to rebel slaves.

The year after Nat Turner and his men were executed, the U.S. Army began to round up the Five Civilized Nations at bayonet point for a forced march to the deserts of Oklahoma. These great Native American nations that once provided a refuge for fugitives in the heart of the South were gone. Even as African-American rebels conspired, they knew their enemies were gaining on them and their escape hatches were disappearing.

The defeats of Prosser, Vesey, and Turner highlighted painful truths. Slaves realized that they were surrounded by southerners who grew up with guns and were capable, in response to resistance, of unlimited racial brutality. Heavily armed militias stood prepared for the first alarm of revolt. Unarmed slaves saw they could be overwhelmed by disciplined, experienced troops with concentrated firepower. "Any attempt at resistance would bring certain and immediate destruction," said slave Lunsford Lane, wise from seeing many uprisings fail.

The men who fought with Prosser, Vesey, and Turner learned that powerful forces waited in distant ambush. Behind local militias stood the awesome military potential of the United States government. Its marching orders came from proslavery politicians.

But the revolutionary upsurges of 1776, 1789, and 1791 fueled black hope and nerve. During Prosser's revolt slaveholders warned that "this new-fangled French revolutionary philosophy of liberty and equality" meant trouble. They called slaves "clearly the Jacobins of the country . . . the Anarchists and the Domestic Enemy." Masters knew that faith in a black liberator, despite all the police and propaganda, was a strong force in slave huts.

The Haitian revolution, as Thomas Jefferson wrote, "appears to have given considerable impulse to the minds of the slaves." Denmark Vesey originally timed his uprising to take place on the French Revolution's Bastille Day. Nat Turner originally chose the Fourth of July. Prosser planned for his armies to carry a banner reading "Liberty or Death," the slogan of liberator L'Ouverture, into Richmond.

Ties of history and blood linked Haiti and enslaved Americans. Prosser, Vesey, and Turner talked of L'Ouverture's military genius and political success. Vesey, one of his men said, "was in the habit of reading to me all the passages in the newspapers that related to San Domingo." For generations Florida's African-American maroons had traded with Haiti. A leader in Louisiana's huge 1811 rebellion was a free black from Haiti, Charles Deslondes.

African insurrections in Haiti, South and Central America, and in the United States sealed the doom of the African slave trade. Between 1807 and 1820, European governments banned the importation of Africans as a threat to white safety. In 1833, England ended bondage in its overseas colonies.

Slave insurrections also created a new problem for slaveholders. In crushing rebels they were forced to reveal the uncharitable and undemocratic character of a system committed to cruelty. With their whips, chains, and fire, they stood exposed as petty and reckless tyrants. To battle their human property, they were fully prepared to undermine both white constitutional rights and the will of the majority.

To protect their investments, slaveholders demanded greater control over Congress and the presidency. They were no longer able to pose as kindly Christian civilizers. Increasingly, they appeared to fellow citizens as a violent force that scoffed at democratic traditions and threatened the peace.

The Fiery Abolitionists

T E N

David Walker was a slim, six-foot black man who made his living running a secondhand clothing store on Brattle Street in Boston. His life's goal was to unite African Americans and overthrow slavery. His radical views fired people with hope and expectation and made slaveholders furious. In a few short years the young African American changed the debate over slavery.

In the 1820s, no one more brilliantly and sharply voiced the anguish and aspirations that more than 2 million slaves shared with their 320,000 free brothers and sisters. Walker knew from his own family that slave and free were as close as husband and wife. He was born in 1785 in Wilmington, North Carolina, to a free black woman married to a slave. His father died before David was born. Slaveholder rules assigned the mother's status to the child, so Walker was born free.

In his late thirties, Walker said farewell to his mother and began to travel. Soon he left the South: "If I remain in this bloody land, I will not live long," he said. "I cannot remain where I must hear the chains." By the time he arrived in Boston in 1827, he had a purpose: "As true as God reigns, I will be avenged for the sorrows which my people have suffered."

At forty, he taught himself to read and write and then began to study history. His consuming interest was the European enslavement of his fellow Africans.

In 1827, *Freedom's Journal*, America's first black newspaper, appeared, and Walker contributed articles and became its Boston distributor. He also attended community meetings and helped runaways reach freedom. He married a woman, probably a fugitive slave, and they hoped to have a child. The next year in a public lecture he asked his people: "Ought we not to . . . protect, aid, and assist each other to the utmost of our power?"

His answer was a lengthy *Appeal to the Slaves of the United States,* published in 1829. Wide-ranging, fiercely militant, and unequivocal in tone, it drew inspiration from his deeply held

David Walker's *Appeal.*

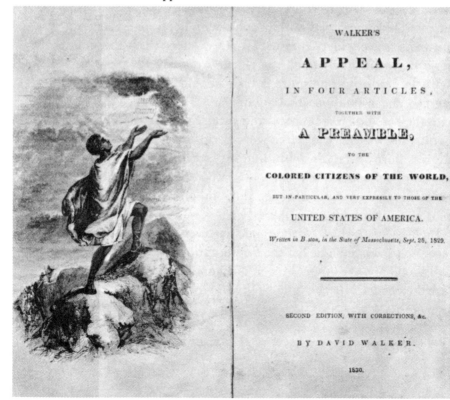

Christian beliefs and the recent democratic spirit that had swept through America, France, and Haiti.

Whites enslaved blacks out of greed, Walker argued, but God had ordained freedom. He "will send you a Hannibal" as leader. He condemned the U.S. government, northern discrimination, and advised his people to prepare "to govern ourselves." At times Walker said white hearts were "so hardened" that they would not repent or apologize, but other times he voiced some hope that slavery could peacefully be ended. "Treat us like men, and . . . we will live in peace and happiness together."

Walker's booklet rang with passionate threats and warnings: "I speak Americans for your own good. We must and shall be free . . . in spite of you." To his people he wrote: "The entire emancipation of your enslaved brethren all over the world" depended on unity among African peoples.

He wished to avoid bloodshed, but at times he coldly calculated the path forward: "Never make an attempt to gain our freedom, or natural right, from under our cruel oppressors and murderers, until you see your way clear—when that hour arrives and you move, be not afraid." "If you commence, make sure work—do not trifle, for they will not trifle with you. . . . kill or be killed." He agreed with Jefferson that people had the right of revolution.

Walker's *Appeal* had an electrifying effect in the South where distribution was probably speeded by sailors Walker had met through his clothing business. In New Orleans, Richmond, and Savannah, African Americans were arrested for owning copies. Legislatures in Georgia, North Carolina, Mississippi, Virginia, and Louisiana imposed a death penalty on anyone circulating materials encouraging slave rebellion. The governor of North Carolina condemned it as "totally subversive . . . an open appeal to natural love of liberty." In Wilmington, Walker's birthplace, authorities reported "unrest and plotting" among African Americans.

The Virginia legislature met in secret session to deal with the

Appeal. Rewards of a thousand dollars or more for Walker's capture or death were offered in Georgia. The mayor of Savannah asked the mayor of Boston to arrest Walker.

To demonstrate support for his *Appeal*, Boston's African-American community toasted Walker at a dinner. "I will stand my ground," he told his friends. "Somebody has to die in this cause. I may be doomed . . . but it is not in me to falter if I can promote the work of emancipation." On the morning of June 28, 1830, Walker was found dead near his home. His friends believed he had been poisoned. Edward, Walker's son, was born soon after.

The white foes of slavery learned from Walker. Originally, Benjamin Lundy, the leading white antislavery voice, condemned the *Appeal* as "bold, daring, inflammatory." His assistant, William Lloyd Garrison, said it was a disaster for the cause. Before Walker appeared, Lundy, Garrison, and other white leaders had urged caution and moderation. They believed that emancipation must be slow, owners should be compensated financially for their loss, and those freed shipped to Africa.

David Walker's bold language changed the argument. By January 1, 1831, when William Lloyd Garrison began his *Liberator*, he had rejected his own earlier, gradual approach and demanded immediate emancipation without any compensation. His words rang with the indignation of a David Walker: "I will not equivocate—I will not excuse—I will not retreat a single inch—AND I WILL BE HEARD." He then launched The American Anti-Slavery Society, which by 1838 claimed 1,346 clubs and a quarter of a million members. It was interracial, militant, and determined.

The first U.S. political effort to include women, the society counted black and white women among its speakers and workers. They faced northern mobs of respectable citizens who broke up meetings 115 times in the 1830s and 64 times in the 1840s.

A former slave who interviewed Walker's wife and reprinted the *Appeal* was Henry Highland Garnet, born in New Market,

Maryland, in 1815. At nine, Garnet walked and—when his legs tired—was carried to freedom by his father and uncle. They lived in New York.

In 1843, at twenty-seven and just married, Garnet was ordained as a Presbyterian minister. At a black convention in Buffalo that year, he issued a call for the solidarity of free and enslaved African Americans and called on slaves to "strike the first blow for freedom." Garnet urged: ". . . rather die freemen, *than live to be slaves.*" He reminded his listeners of the heroism of Denmark Vesey, Nat Turner, Joseph Cinqué, and Madison Washington and concluded: "Brethren, arise, arise! Strike for your lives and liberties. Now is the day and the hour. Let every slave throughout the land do this, and the days of slavery are numbered."

When his speech was offered as a resolution, it failed by a single vote in Buffalo. Approving it, some feared, would unleash lynch mobs against black families in southern states. But Garnet issued his *Address to the Slaves of the United States* that year in a pamphlet that also included Walker's *Appeal.*

Because of Walker's *Appeal* and Garnet's *Address,* resistance to slavery became highly organized in black northern communities. Beginning in 1830, annual national conventions were organized by ex-slaves to direct campaigns against slavery and discrimination. By then, fifty black societies were sponsoring protest meetings and issuing publications, including "slave narratives" that exposed the horrors of slavery to the reading public.

The words of Walker and Garnet helped stir militant responses to oppression among African Americans. From New York to California the arrest of runaways increasingly triggered community mobilization. In 1833, when Mr. and Mrs. Thornton Blackburn of Detroit were seized as Kentucky slaves, the community sprang into action. A jailhouse visitor secretly changed clothes with Mrs. Blackburn, who walked out of her cell and was ferried to Canada. The sheriff who returned Mr. Blackburn to slavery was attacked and his skull fractured.

William Lambert and George DeBaptiste formed a secret Detroit escape network called African-American Mysteries: The Order of the Men of Oppression. "The general plan was freedom," explained Lambert, and his determined band "arranged passwords and grips, and a ritual, but we were always suspicious of the white man, and so those we admitted we put to severe tests." "It was fight and run—danger at every turn, but that we calculated upon, and were prepared for," he recalled.

In Cass County, Michigan, four fugitives from Kentucky were arrested and brought to South Bend, Indiana. Black and white citizens demanded the posse's arrest, and black residents with clubs and guns massed across from the court. In two days the four were released and carried off in triumph.

On June 3, 1847, a Pennsylvania community swung into action. The *Carlisle Herald* reported "an attempt on the part of a large portion of our colored population to rescue several slaves who had been arrested as fugitives." As a man, woman, and young girl were led from the court, people lunged and a battle "ensued in the street . . . paving stones were hurled in showers, and clubs and canes used." The woman and girl escaped, but the man was taken back to Maryland.

That year in Troy, New York, a black national convention recommended instructing "sons in the art of war." Black conventions were meeting annually to plan ways to combat slavery and discrimination.

In 1850, Congress passed a new Fugitive Slave Law that imposed severe penalties for aiding runaways, denied the accused any right to testify, and required citizens to help catch runaways. Slavery's violence spilled into northern streets. Whites who had believed that slavery would not touch them now faced jail and fines if they refused to follow the commands of slave-hunters.

Black communities prepared for battle. Former slave the Reverend Jarmain Loguen announced, "I don't respect this law—I don't fear it—I won't obey it! It outlaws me and I outlaw it."

Fugitive Lewis Hayden, who hid runaways in his Boston home, announced he had placed two kegs of explosives in his basement and would blow up the house rather than surrender to anyone.

In Boston, Cleveland, and Detroit, black vigilance committees expanded to meet the threat, and in Philadelphia, Albany, Syracuse, and New York City, integrated committees also signed up new members. Cleveland's committee of four women and five men helped 275 escapees in eight months. In Springfield, Massachusetts, an armed League of Gileadites, forty-four men and women, mostly black, pledged to arm against slavery, and to be "firm, determined and cool" and "be hanged, if you must."

Slave-hunters rode into the North and civilian forces were deployed and ready. In February, in the first case under the new law, Fred Wilkins, a fugitive living in Boston, found he had neighbors willing to help and Lewis Hayden had organized them.

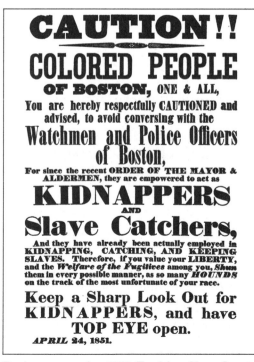

Resistance to the 1850 Fugitive Slave Law
began to unite black and white northerners.

Richard Henry Dana wrote: "We heard a shout from the Court House" as "two huge negroes, bearing the prisoner between them, with his clothes half torn off" rushed him away "like a black squall, the crowd driving along with them and cheering as they went." In Syracuse, New York, a mixed force of blacks and whites stormed into a courthouse and liberated fugitive Jerry McHenry.

William Parker had escaped to Christiana, Pennsylvania, and trained a small black army to wage war on slave-hunters. Warned that a federal posse was headed his way to seize two fugitives hiding in his house, Parker and his men loaded their weapons, sang "Die on the Field of Battle, Glory in My Soul," and waited. On the morning of September 11, Maryland slaveholder Edward Gorsuch, his son, and a U.S. marshal and his deputies arrived at Parker's fortresslike home. When the lawmen called for surrender, Parker and his men laughed.

Parker's wife sounded a horn from the second-floor window, and dozens of armed blacks—nobody knows to this day how many—appeared. Gunfire broke out, and when the smoke had cleared, Gorsuch lay dead, his son seriously wounded, and Parker's army and friends were racing to Canada.

The U.S. government dispatched forty-five Marines to Christiana and tried thirty-six blacks and two Quakers for treason. All were acquitted. The battle at Christiana announced that African Americans were ready to fight for liberty.

In Boston, the arrest of Anthony Burns in 1854 had the Reverend Thomas W. Higginson, a noted reformer, abolitionist, and writer, lead a black and white assault unit on the courthouse. They killed a deputy, but were repulsed by overwhelming force. It took twenty-two U.S. military units to hold back angry, shouting Boston crowds and return Burns to the South.

These efforts to rescue fugitives in the 1850s drew white support and began to change national thinking. Recalled the Reverend Mr. Higginson, "Brought up as we have all been, it takes the

William Parker and his armed forces drive off a U.S. marshal and his posse.

whole experience of one such case to educate the mind to the attitude of revolution." He found it "so strange to find one's self outside of established institutions," to lower one's voice and hide one's purposes, "to see law and order, police and military on the wrong side, and find good citizenship a sin and bad citizenship a duty."

Some clashes were more clever than explosive. In 1853, Louis, a fugitive on trial in a Cincinnati court, pushed his chair back, then stepped backward. A white abolitionist touched his foot to encourage him, and Louis kept inching back. He quietly backed around the room and someone put a hat on his head. When he reached the black section, people crowded around and rushed him through the door. Abolitionists dressed Louis in women's clothes and hurried him to freedom.

At times abolitionists used both legal and illegal means to rescue fugitives. In May 1857, some fired on a U.S. marshal and posse of ten who tried to break into a Mechanicsburg, Ohio, home. The lawmen fled. At nearby Lumbarton another posse was arrested by citizens who charged they were using unnecessary force. A conference between Governor Chase and President Buchanan had to settle the case's complex legal conflicts.

In 1858, a black and white strike force from Oberlin, Ohio, rescued black fugitive John Price from a posse that included two U.S. marshals. Of the thirty-seven rescuers arrested, two were tried. One, Charles Langston, spoke so strongly about an African American's right to challenge the new law—"I will do all I can for any man thus seized and held"—that the judge gave him a minimum sentence.

In 1859, Harriet Tubman helped liberate Charles Nalle from lawmen in Troy, New York. For half an hour, her black and white civilian band battled Nalle's captors as she fastened a grip on him and held it while clubs struck her head. When the male rescuers were wounded, black women, she reported, "rushed over their bodies, brought Nalle out," and sped him to safety.

Some African-American women taken west as slaves sued for freedom in court. In San Jose, California, Mary brought a case in 1846 and won her liberty. In the next decade, in Los Angeles, Biddy Mason gained liberty for herself and three daughters with the help of a local sheriff. During a San Francisco dispute over a fugitive, the African-American community raised such a furor that state legislators wanted to register them and ban any future black migration. In 1852, Robbin and Polly Holmes, who had gained their freedom, brought suit in Oregon for the liberty of their three children and won the case.

The Fugitive Slave Law set North against South. It made some northern whites wonder if owners of slaves might be trying to control all of the United States. By sending southern posses racing through the streets of northern cities and towns, slaveholders triggered anger from those who thought they were untouched by or neutral about slavery.

Insisting the Constitution protected them from being forced into slave-hunting posses, all free-state legislatures except New Jersey and California passed Personal Liberty Laws. This legislation represented the first major legal defeat for the slaveholders of the United States.

Slaveholders found the northern resistance to the law intolerable, in the words of the Augusta, Georgia, *Republican,* "a successful farce." It summarized the case of a fugitive named Sims. Sims was kept in court for a week, a police detachment was necessary, and "the building was surrounded by a barricade of chains, and hundreds of the military had to be kept on guard to prevent his forcible rescue." Slave-hunters were jailed for kidnapping and released only on bail of up to $10,000. Finally, "one of the agents narrowly escaped being struck on the head by a Negro named Randolph." This conduct, complained the *Republican,* will prevent masters from "attempting to regain their slaves."

In the 1850s, slaves increasingly heard news about the rising conflicts between North and South. By 1856, slaveholders reported their slaves were excited by the birth of a Republican Party dedicated to banning slavery in the West, and its presidential candidate, John Frémont. That year slaves also learned that whites in Kansas fought in armed battles over the future of bondage. A journalist in Kansas wrote: "The slaves are in a state of insurrection all over the country."

Slaves in the South escaped in larger numbers than ever before, and more whites, particularly the poor, aided them and took part in slave conspiracies. Panicky talk of black insurrections was heard in several states.

The Washington correspondent for the *New York Weekly Tribune* wrote in 1856 that "the insurrectionary movement in Tennessee" made "more headway than is known to the public" and insisted "important facts [were] being suppressed in order to check the spread of the contagion." The next week he told of serious outbreaks in New Orleans, though local papers "carefully refrain from any mention of the facts."

The *New Orleans Picayune* admitted it "refrained from publishing a great deal" about the "spirit of turbulence." Two weeks later the *Picayune* said Christmas fires pointed to "slave plots" in

Kentucky, Arkansas, Tennessee, Mississippi, Louisiana, and Texas. Its evidence added up to a "positive insurrection."

That year in Colorado County, Texas, two hundred rebellious slaves were helped, it was reported, by "the lower class of the Mexican population." By the presidential election in November, slaves in southwestern Texas had hatched a plot in three counties to murder tracking hounds and "prepare for a general attack."

In Mexico, reporter Olmsted found, "Runaways were *constantly* arriving." He found that "two had got over the night before . . . forty . . . in the last three months. At other points, further down the [Rio Grande] river, a great many more came than here." So many had escaped, he found, that their Texas owners agreed to pardon any that returned voluntarily. Mexico, he wrote, had thousands of free African Americans.

Fugitives from border states slipped across the Mason-Dixon line in large numbers. When the Ohio River froze, so many Kentucky runaways crossed the ice that congestion became a problem. So many fugitives crowded into underground railroad stations in Lawrence, Kansas, in 1859, that its director, Colonel J. Bowles, desperately called for large amounts of financial aid.

The 1850s witnessed massive efforts to help escapees, including Harriet Tubman's nineteen trips. Jane Lewis went to Kentucky to help fugitives cross the river to freedom. Escapees Elizah Anderson and John Mason rescued more than two thousand. Mason was captured and sold back into slavery, but he escaped and continued his work. Former slave Arnold Cragston spent four years rowing hundreds from Kentucky across the Ohio River, saying, "We just knew there was a lot of slaves always a-wantin' to get free, and I had to help 'em."

The conflict between slaves and owners had moved to center stage by the 1850s. Fear of a Nat Turner or Toussaint L'Ouverture had planters demanding that all whites commit themselves to slave control. These owners controlled their state governments.

Slaveholder contempt for democracy and the rights of all leaped the boundaries of the South. They won the right to ban antislavery literature from the southern mail system. They set bonfires of suspected abolitionist material outside of southern post offices. In 1831, a southern paper threatened the lives of northern abolitionists "upon all occasions which may place them in our power." In 1836, southerners in Congress won a "gag rule" that banned any petitions about slavery. It took an eight-year battle for congressmen to lift this ban. To tighten their control over slaves, masters had to demand new laws and compromises from northerners in Congress and out.

The abolitionist movement, inspired by slave resistance and determined to end the system one way or another, became increasingly revolutionary. By the 1850s, thousands of its black and white men and women members were helping runaways escape, challenging federal efforts to return fugitives, and discussing slavery's violent overthrow in the South.

On abolition's cutting edge was John Brown, a man of action. A devout Christian who identified fully with African Americans, he planned to seize the federal arsenal at Harpers Ferry, Virginia (later West Virginia), and help launch black maroon colonies in the Alleghenies. Brown told Frederick Douglass these mountains were placed by God "to aid the emancipation of your race." Douglass admired Brown's courage but warned him he was heading into a "perfect steel trap."

On October 16, 1859, Brown led a band of twenty-two that included five blacks and seventeen whites, including his own sons. Two black recruits had been charged in the Oberlin rescue: John Copeland, an Oberlin student, and Copeland's uncle, Lewis Sheridan Leary (an ancestor of poet Langston Hughes).

U.S. troops commanded by Col. Robert E. Lee and Lt. J. E. B. Stuart trapped Brown and his men. Ten were killed, seven (including Brown) were captured, and five escaped. However, the assault proved some whites were willing to die fighting slavery.

Above: The capture of John Brown.

Below: John Brown before the court in Charleston.

The quiet courage and thoughtful words of Brown during the forty days before his execution stirred the world and placed emancipation on the national agenda. In France, Victor Hugo called him "an apostle and a hero" and a "martyr." Poet James Russell Lowell said: "But that scaffold sways the future."

In 1860, President Lincoln and the Republican Party won the presidency. Those who owned slaves no longer dictated U.S. policy. Eleven southern states threatened to secede from the Union and form their own confederacy. Bishop Elliot of Savannah announced that self-government and equality were "great falsehoods." Confederate vice president Alexander H. Stephens's inauguration speech called slavery "the great truth" and stated that "freedom is not possible without slavery."

Once slaveholders claimed they were pious, democratic gentlemen. They still felt that way about themselves. But in 1861, many northerners realized slaveholders were far more committed to slavery than democracy. To protect slavery they would ignore rights for which Americans had fought and died.

Marching to Freedom

The Slaves' Civil War

ELEVEN

In the four months between Lincoln's election and his inauguration as president of the United States, South Carolina, Mississippi, Florida, Alabama, Georgia, Louisiana, and Texas formed the southern Confederacy. They elected their own president and began to seize the federal forts and arsenals on their lands.

Slaves from Virginia to Florida and Texas watched the growing hostility among whites for sparks that could ignite their freedom. One December night, sixty slaves marched through New Castle, Kentucky, singing political songs, shouting Republican slogans. Said a Texan: "We sleep upon our arms and the whole country is deeply excited."

In Natchez, Mississippi, an African American named Mosley and other slaves planned a rebellion on March 4, Lincoln's inauguration day. Mosley was seized and confessed: "I said, 'Lincoln would set us free.' Alfred and Monroe Harris proposed a company to be raised. Drago has a pistol to shoot master. I got two pistols from Bill Chamberlain. Bill has a fine shooter pistol. I heard Harvey say Obey would join us. Howard told Margaret he murdered the Dutchman. Harry and Alfred are all for the plan."

Mosley and his followers proved unduly optimistic about the new president. Lincoln, though he personally hated bondage, stated his aim was to save the Union and not interfere with the South's "internal institutions." He reassured all Americans, "If I could save the union without freeing any slave, I would do it."

But by the end of March 1861, eight runaways reached Fort Pickering, Florida, expecting federal officers to recognize the liberty they had seized. They were turned away. That summer, a Bowling Green, Kentucky, owner said his slaves "know too much about Lincoln. . . . It is too late now; they know as much as we do, and too much for our safety and peace of mind."

Following the Confederate firing on Fort Sumter in April, hysteria over slave unrest swept Arkansas, Texas, Mississippi, Alabama, Louisiana, and Tennessee. A Mississippi master spoke of the "possibility of an insurrection," and attempts "to poison and . . . burn houses." By May, a white wrote of slave defiance in New Orleans—"slavery requires armed power to keep it in order," "very alarming disturbances among the blacks," and on more than one plantation "open resistance." When "a dozen ships were burned at anchor in New Orleans early in May," whites told a reporter "slaves were responsible."

African Americans in South Carolina and Mississippi exhibited a new mood. Mary Chestnut sensed it her house slaves. A butler, whom she had taught to read, was "inscrutably silent" and "won't look at me now. He looks over my head, he scents freedom in the air."

In July, W. B. Williams complained to Mississippi governor Pettus, "I cannot manage my negroes myself and they are bad." In October, owner Addie Harris insisted it was "dangerous to leave them by themselves." In December, slaves were blamed for a Charleston fire that destroyed six hundred buildings.

When white men left for the Confederate army, southern food crops were neglected. Slaves saw that fewer whites were in control. Planters informed Governor Pettus that no more young men could be spared for the front because "now we have to patrol every night." Whites complained about black "insolence" and of slaves who "won't work." Talking of his own and his sister's plantations, Addie Harris said: "Her negroes as well as mine are very near free and I cannot get my crop gathered."

The Confederate Congress passed a law that allowed overseers to avoid the draft. The poorer whites who owned no slaves claimed it was "a rich man's war and a poor man's fight." At a time when the Confederacy desperately needed unity, this created bitterness between two important groups of whites.

Planters were infuriated by new laws permitting the Confederacy to draft slaves for labor on fortifications. This war work opened a new horizon for slaves who had never before left the plantation. They made contacts with free blacks who were also drafted, worked close to Union lines, and learned about roads, rivers, and firearms. Some began to study troop movements.

They watched in amazement as officers shouted at each other and argued with their owners. They never witnessed so much white division, and it was growing. War had always made slaves an undependable labor force, but this one, they began to feel, was really about their own liberty.

Union rifle fire often missed Confederate targets, but it tore huge holes in the institution of slavery. With armed foes nearby, masters no longer enjoyed unlimited power over those in chains. As Union guns spoke in the distance, slaves shirked duties, resisted orders, and scoffed at authority. As they learned the lay of the land, flight became easier. Some slaves fled home to gather up their families and race to freedom.

What had been the Confederacy's biggest asset now became its worst problem—an enemy within during wartime. "They deserted at every opportunity," said both white officers and civilians.

The Union announced it opposed slave resistance. General

George McClellan declared, "We will, with an iron hand, crush any attempt at insurrection," and General Ben Butler issued a similar order. McClellan expelled the Hutchinson family folk-singers from his camp for singing antislavery songs.

New York African-American editor Thomas Hamilton predicted: "The forlorn hope of insurrection among the slaves may as well be abandoned. They are too well informed and too wise to court destruction at the hands of the combined Northern and Southern armies."

In May 1861, as slave laborers continued to flee the Confederates and seek refuge in Union lines, a change of policy began. General Butler at Fort Monroe, Virginia, declared slaves "contraband of war" and refused to return any to rebel owners. With this terse military phrase the process of emancipation began. In two months Fort Monroe had 900 fugitives, 3,000 by Christmas.

Now thousands of African Americans made their way to Union lines. The slaveholders' claims that their laborers were a docile, happy people faded with each batch of arrivals. For their escape some had stolen horses or buggies, boats, rafts, or canoes.

But freedom was not official U.S. policy, and people not only had to escape the Confederacy, eluding soldiers and slave patrols, but they had to reach Union officers who would not return them. For example, in February 1862, U.S. General Buell ordered slaves returned, but his junior officers quietly promised protection to any carrying military information. They declared slaves "our only friends."

In the face of a confused Union policy, many runaways preferred to remain in no-man's-land between the lines. Entire families or colonies of runaways lived between a foe they hated and an ally they could not trust.

But still they fled. General Burnside reported in March 1862 from New Bern, North Carolina: "They find their way to us through woods and swamp from every side," and once within federal lines, were "wild with excitement and delight."

Above: Slaves begin to leave Hampton, Virginia, plantations for freedom as "contrabands" at Fort Monroe.

Below: Slaves entering Fort Monroe.

The Union forces gained valuable information from those fleeing Confederate fortifications and war work. In April, Confederate Commander Thomas Jones reported from Pensacola that "the greatest trouble" was fugitives racing to the enemy with valuable information about his troop strength.

In North Carolina, a Confederate officer estimated that by August 1862, a million dollars in slaves fled the Confederacy each week. As the South lost laborers, bluecoats gained willing volunteers. Over campfires, after battle, young white soldiers taught black refugees the magic of reading and writing.

In Florida, where the biracial Seminoles had battled slavehunters for decades, black guerrilla units roamed. In April 1862, Confederate Brigadier General Floyd asked Florida governor Milton "as a measure of absolute necessity" to declare martial law in six counties in the war against "traitors and lawless negroes."

A South Carolina paper reported "from five to six hundred negroes" in two counties were "roving the country." "Guerrilla warfare," it said, was threatening southern meat supplies. Edmund Ruffin, the slaveholder who fired the first cannon at Fort Sumter, became worried about slave insurrections. He wrote in his diary about something "I never did before . . . keeping loaded guns by my bedside." He described a Virginia conspiracy, hatched at "night meetings for pretended religious worship," and concluded "we ought to be always vigilant," ready to repel attacks from "northern invaders or negro insurgents."

In November 1861, a Union fleet captured Port Royal in the Georgia and South Carolina Sea Islands. U.S. General Rufus Saxton reported thousands of former slaves were ready to work for the Union. They had fought their owners to stay and to welcome the invaders:

They tried to take their negroes with them [deeper into Confederate territory], but they would not go. They shot down their negroes in many instances because they would not go with them. They tied

them behind their wagons and tried to drag them off; but the negroes
would not go. The great majority of negroes [80 percent] remained
behind and came into our lines.

The southern countryside was filled with slaves fleeing or
hiding supplies of arms, gunpowder, and knives. A Confederate
officer wrote to Governor Pettus of widespread slave resistance
and flight, adding· "Within the last 12 months we have had to
hang some 40 for plotting an insurrection, and there has been
about that number put in irons."

Black troops, former slaves, guard a Sea Islands mansion in 1862.

In April 1862, the Union fleet and army captured New Orleans. General Butler met with officers of the Louisiana Native Guards, blacks whom Confederates had enlisted. They had been trained, not with guns but with broomsticks, and never sent into battle. The officers told Butler their soldiers would like to exchange broomsticks for rifles and would be happy to fight for the Union. Butler at first refused, but agreed to arm them when a Confederate army appeared in the neighborhood.

By September, Louisiana masters close to Union lines were complaining of field hands that some "would not work at all, and others wanted wages." On the Magnolia plantation, the owner cried, "We have a terrible state of affairs here . . . negroes refusing to work." His laborers built a gallows and said they "will be free" only after they drive off or "hang their master."

The Union presence in Louisiana offered the slave population new choices. The U.S. flags at Fort Parapet four miles north of New Orleans, or at Fort Jackson and Fort Philip at the mouth of the Mississippi, became more than banners of liberty. Slaves south of the city stayed on plantations and won concessions of $10 a month in wages and no use of whips. Others, who left their owners but were unable to reach federal lines, chose a new life in maroon colonies in swamps and bayou underbrush. When planters abandoned land, many slaves waited to see which white side offered them better choices.

One of the most unusual wartime escapes was planned by Robert Smalls, the slave pilot of the Confederate battleship *Planter*, and his black crew. On the evening of May 13, 1862, after the white captain and officers left the ship, Smalls and his African-American crew picked up their families and loved ones on the shore. Smalls blinked the correct signal at Confederate-held Fort Sumter, sailed out of Charleston harbor at 4:00 A.M., and surrendered to the Union Navy. "I thought the *Planter* might be of some use to Uncle Abe," he said with a smile. Smalls was the first man to steal a battleship, and living proof that slaves only waited for the opportunity to help the Union. For the rest of the war, Smalls served the U.S. Navy as captain of the *Planter*.

Other African Americans fled with guts, faith, and little else. One said, "We thought freedom better than clothes, so we left them." A slave of eighty-eight who ran said, "Never too old for leave de land o' bondage." An elderly couple, Si and his ill wife, ran off, but she died in the woods. When his owner asked Si why they tried so hazardous a trip, he answered, "I couldn't help it, marster, but then, you see, she died free." Two Louisiana families with children on their backs spent two days and nights wading in mud and water to reach Union lines. A Georgia woman placed her twenty-two children and grandchildren on a raft and floated to the Yankees.

A slave family who rode into Union lines appears in a Mathew Brady photograph.

Masters and mistresses were shocked to find both loyal and hostile slaves had abandoned them. Emily Douglass of Natchez always boasted of her slaves' undying loyalty, but now: "They left without even a good-bye."

"One life they show their masters and another life they don't show," Robert Smalls had said.

Emma Holmes refused to believe blacks had become so unruly and blamed Yankees for exciting "the foulest demoniac passions of the negro, hitherto so peaceful and happy."

Some whites tried not only to accept painful truths, but to act on their new knowledge. Alexander Jones, a Hendersonville, North Carolina, spokesman for poor whites, now realized the wealthy planters had ruled by dividing "negroes and poor helpless whites." His "Heroes of America" with ten thousand members sided with the North. When some were arrested and forced into the Wilmington salt mines alongside slave laborers, they helped many African-American fellow prisoners reach Union lines.

Because the war did not end in ninety days as both sides had predicted, President Lincoln faced trouble on the political warfront. Drafting whites into the Union Army led to so much violence in New York City, Pennsylvania, Ohio, Indiana, and Wisconsin that federal troops were rushed to these states. Federal marshals arrested and jailed without trial five newspaper editors, three judges, antiwar politicians, and hundreds of antidraft rioters.

On the battlefield, both sides continued to suffer staggering casualties, and there was no sign of victory. By the end of 1862, 100,000 Union soldiers had deserted their posts.

Abolitionists and northern newspapers constantly pointed out that as whites bled and died for the Union, southerners whipped blacks into bringing in their crops and building their forts. In

February 1862, a *New York Times* reporter in liberated Port Royal wrote that everywhere "blacks hurry in droves to our lines; they crowd in small boats around our ships; they swarm upon our decks; they hurry to our officers from the cotton houses of their masters, an hour or two after the guns are fired."

African-American men and women in U.S. lines represented an enormous potential as laborers, spies, and soldiers. For freedom, they would eagerly wield shovels or rifles. Parents of Union soldiers and northern papers no longer ignored these facts.

Under such pressure, antislavery views gained in the North. In the winter and spring of 1862, fiery abolitionist orator Wendell Phillips was suddenly flooded with lecture invitations. In a Washington, D.C., he had dared not enter a year before, he was invited to address large assemblies that included President Lincoln and members of Congress. Vice President Hamlin personally introduced his booming, radical voice to the U.S. Senate.

The president feared that freeing slaves would cost him the support of the four loyal border slave states and lose him many votes in the 1864 election. He was right. But Congress believed that unless radical action was taken, the North could lose the war. Congressmen were determined to draw off the South's slaves one way or another and arm them. It rejected as impractical Lincoln's plans to pay owners who freed slaves and to have the government resettle liberated people in another country. Congress rushed past Lincoln toward immediate emancipation, without either compensation to owners or deportation of blacks.

By July 1862, Congress prohibited Union officers from returning anyone to Confederate owners. It authorized the president to enlist "persons of African descent" for "any war service." Confiscation of slaves as property, it said, was just punishment for traitors. African Americans who entered Union lines, it voted, "shall be deemed captives of war and shall be forever free."

Congress was trying to catch up with the reality hundreds of

By May 1863, thousands of African Americans were pouring into Union lines.

thousands of black feet had already created. Their daring flights to Union lines and offers to help defeat the Confederacy put emancipation on the national agenda. The refusal by U.S. officers in the field to return them, and finally Congress's dry legalities, ratified what the slaves had accomplished. Emancipation needed only the president's signature.

As slaves poured into Union lines, the president cautiously stepped forward to catch up with them, Congress, and events. On July 13, 1862, Lincoln told navy secretary Gideon Welles he was going to issue an emancipation proclamation. He believed that slavery was "at the heart of the rebellion" and freedom had "occupied his mind and thoughts day and night." Emancipation, he decided, was "a military necessity, absolutely essential to the preservation of the Union. We must free the slaves or be ourselves subdued. The slaves were undeniably an element of strength to those who had their service, and we must decide whether that element should be with us or against us."

On July 22, Lincoln told his cabinet of the decision and won their approval. After the Union victory at Antietam in September, he announced his preliminary proclamation. If the Confederacy did not surrender by the first day of 1863, the president would issue a final proclamation freeing all slaves of rebels.

In stiff, official language, the Emancipation Proclamation freed only slaves in regions still in rebellion—where masters held power. It did not liberate the 450,000 in Delaware, Kentucky, Maryland, and Missouri, or the 275,000 in occupied Tennessee, and the tens of thousands in the Union-ruled portions of Louisiana and Virginia. It short, it liberated people in areas controlled by the Confederacy.

But the proclamation also was a declaration that every Confederate-owned African American who reached Union lines was free. Lincoln also invited these "freedmen" (as they were called) to enlist in the Union armed forces. The president again was catching up with history, for African Americans had been quietly enrolled in and fighting for the U.S. Army in Louisiana, Kansas, and along the coastline in Georgia and South Carolina.

African-American communities celebrated emancipation on January 1, 1863. At Boston's Tremont Temple at midnight a black minister led the singing of "Jehovah has triumphed, his people are free." In a camp for fugitives near the White House, a man whose daughter had been sold said, "Now, no more dat! . . . Dey can't sell my wife and child anymore, bless de Lord!"

"Brothers! The hour strikes for us," wrote a black New Orleans paper in French and English. Frederick Douglass said: "The day dawns—the morning star is bright upon the horizon."

On the Sea Islands, men who had already carried the war to their former owners gathered for emancipation ceremonies. Charlotte Forten, a black New England schoolteacher, was present: "I wish it were possible to describe fitly the scene which met our eyes as we sat upon the stand and looked down on the crowd before us. There were black soldiers in their blue coats, and scarlet pantaloons, the officers of this and other regiments in their handsome uniforms, and crowds of lookers-on—men, women and children of every complexion, grouped in various attitudes under the moss-hung trees."

Colonel Thomas W. Higginson, who had helped rescue captured fugitives in Boston, was their commander. As the colors were presented to the troops, there was an unplanned climax. Higginson wrote:

The very moment the speaker had ceased, and just as I took and waved the flag, which now for the first time meant anything to these poor people, there suddenly arose, close beside the platform, a strong male voice (but rather cracked and elderly), into which two women's voices instantly blended, singing, as if by an impulse that could not more be repressed than the morning note of the song-sparrow—

> *My country, 'tis of thee,*
> *Sweet land of liberty,*
> *Of thee I sing!*

People looked at each other, and then at us on the platform, to see whence came this interruption, not set down on the bills. Firmly and irrepressibly, the quavering voices sang on, verse after verse; others of the colored people joined in; some whites on the platform began, but I motioned them to silence. I never saw anything so electric; it made all other words cheap; it seemed the choked voice of a race at last unloosed. . . . Just think of it!—the first day they had ever had a country, the first flag they had ever seen which promised anything to their people, and here, while mere spectators stood in silence, waiting for my stupid words, these simple souls burst out in their lay, as if they were by their own hearths at home!

Colonel Thomas W. Higginson (center) and Sergeant Prince Rivers (left).

The Bayonets of Freedom

TWELVE

"Liberty won by white men," said Frederick Douglass, "would lose half its luster." In the name of Denmark Vesey, Nat Turner, and John Brown, Douglass summoned his people: "Men of Color, To Arms! To Arms!" "By every consideration which binds you to your enslaved fellow countrymen, and the peace and welfare of your country; by every aspiration which you cherish for the freedom and equality of yourselves and your children; by the ties of blood and identity which unite us with the black men now fighting our battles in Louisiana and in South Carolina, I urge you to fly to arms, and smite with death the power that would bury the government and your liberty in the same hopeless grave."

Henry Highland Garnet and William Wells Brown joined him in a committee to direct recruiting. Douglass became an adviser to President Lincoln.

As African Americans flocked to enlist, white northerners and southerners scoffed at the idea of their being able to fight. A northern missionary on the Sea Islands said: "I don't believe you could make soldiers of these men at all—they are afraid, and they know it." A southern paper claimed: "The idea of their doing any serious fighting against white men is simply ridiculous." Less than a year before his proclamation, President Lincoln said: "If we are to arm them, I fear that in a few weeks the arms would be in the hands of the rebels."

After centuries of racial propaganda, the first major test of equality would be on the battlefield. "If slaves make good soldiers, then our whole theory of slavery is wrong," said Confederate General Howell Cobb. The Confederate Congress knew he was right. Late in the war it discussed recruiting slaves, but steadfastly refused to train or arm them.

Most northerners were as strongly infected as slaveholders with a belief in black inferiority and bitterly resented fighting for black liberation. Northern whites feared freed slaves would settle in the North and by working for less pay, take their jobs. This

A young man who fought for freedom—his own and his people's.

fear of emancipation and an unpopular military draft led to city rioting by the poor and uneducated. In New York City, a draft riot lasted for four days as white mobs burned black homes and lynched blacks in the streets. U.S. troops recalled from the battle of Gettysburg had to quell a slaughter that left hundreds dead.

Emancipation had to be tested in fire, and a lot was riding on its success or failure. Black success on the battlefield would determine white willingness to grant citizenship and equality after the war. There was also an immediate political consequence. Unless African Americans proved courageous soldiers, President Lincoln might face defeat in 1864's national election.

The news from the battlefield soon stilled the doubts. The army's new recruits bravely attacked heavily armed foes and doggedly defended their positions. On May 27, former Louisiana slaves faced deadly artillery fire as they charged over open ground toward a Confederate stronghold at Port Hudson. On June 7, a thousand African-American soldiers, so recently enrolled they had not finished their training, used bayonets to push back a Confederate army twice their size. On July 18, the 54th Massachusetts, a black regiment that included Frederick Douglass's son, demonstrated grit and daring in a charge against a heavily fortified position at Fort Wagner. Facing heavy casualties, they were forced to retreat. But their heroism won them admiration and unstinting praise in the North.

On August 26, 1863, President Lincoln, based on reports from his commanders in the field, declared that "the emancipation policy and the use of colored troops constitute the heaviest blow yet dealt the rebellion." These black troops, he wrote, "with silent tongue, and clenched teeth, and a steady eye, and well-poised bayonet" have "helped mankind."

Before the war ended, 178,958 black men took part in 449 engagements and 39 major battles. More than a fifth of all black males under forty-five served in the Union Army and comprised

The battlefield bravery of the 54th Massachusetts helped to convince Lincoln that black troops could be depended on.

a tenth of the U.S. land forces. Some 29,511 African Americans served in the U.S. Navy, meaning every fourth sailor was black.

These African-American volunteers arrived as both sides began to exhaust their supply of reserves. Without his black troops, President Lincoln wrote in August 1864, "we would be compelled to abandon the war in 3 weeks."

At sea and on land, twenty-two African Americans earned the newly minted Congressional Medal of Honor. U.S. General Daniel Ullman interviewed hundreds of his soldiers and found they "are far more earnest than we." He concluded, "They understand their position full as well as we do" and know "that if we are unsuccessful, they will be remanded to a worse slavery than before."

From the moment they enlisted, black soldiers faced greater dangers than whites. Their training period was short, their guns

Some 179,000 black soldiers served in the army. An even larger number of black men, women, and children helped in Union camps as laborers.

and medical supplies inferior, their hospitals and doctors few. Many were marched to the front woefully unprepared, and some were used as shock troops to soften up the foe for white soldiers. For these reasons, 37,300 black men lost their lives, a casualty rate far surpassing that of white troops.

White officers began by scoffing at their intelligence, doubting their fighting capacity, and questioning their battle readiness. The U.S. government treated them as inferior by denying them black officers and by paying them half the wages given white soldiers.

The Confederacy announced that black soldiers and their white officers would be treated as slave rebels and executed when captured. This danger turned African Americans into what General Ullman called "daring and desperate fighters."

The threat was carried out. "The men were perfectly exasperated at the idea of negroes opposed to them & rushed at them like so many devils," wrote a Confederate private, describing a massacre that followed a surrender. At Fort Pillow, on April 12, 1864, Confederate General Nathan Bedford Forrest's troops massacred black prisoners by locking them in houses that were then set on fire. After the war Forrest became the leader of the Ku Klux Klan. The atrocities finally ended when Lincoln threatened retaliation against Confederate prisoners.

Dramatic changes in social relations rocked the South by 1863.

Colonel Thomas W. Higginson, who commanded the First South Carolina Volunteers, said his troops ranked among the best in the army: "Their superiority lies simply in the fact that they know the country, which white troops do not; and, moreover, that they have peculiarities of temperament, position, and motive, which belong to them alone. Instead of leaving their homes and families to fight, they are fighting for their homes and families; and they show the resolution and sagacity which a personal purpose gives. It would have been madness to attempt with the bravest white troops what I have successfully accomplished with black ones."

Higginson was one of many officers who relied on African Americans as spies. "They have been spies all their lives. You cannot teach them anything in that respect." Allan Pinkerton of the Union Secret Service found them "invaluable." To gather vital data for Pinkerton, John Scobel, an ex-slave, repeatedly crossed into enemy lines.

A slave serving as a spy for the Union armies.

Confederates could do little but complain that every slave was a potential spy. A Southern clergyman called slaves "traitors who may pilot an enemy into your bedchamber! They know every road and swamp and creek and plantation in the county." In 1864, a Confederate officer insisted slaves were "an omnipresent spy system, pointing out our valuable men to the enemy, revealing our positions, purposes, and resources and yet acting so safely and secretly that there is no means to guard against it."

Confederates also had to deal with slaves who provided crucial aid to Union soldiers trapped behind their lines or held in prisons. "To see a black face was to find a true heart," said one escapee. A prisoner told this story: "Sometimes forty negroes, male and female, would come to us from one plantation, each one bringing something to give and lay at our feet."

African-American communities inside the Confederacy formed networks to aid escapees. "Knowing no one in the city [Charleston]," two white fugitives from a Confederate stockade recalled, "we relied upon the negroes." They were provided a hideout for two months, and then guided to Union lines.

Private John Ransom and several fellow prisoners were led by black guides, even through a Confederate fortress, and over sleeping soldiers. Ransom recalled: "The negroes were fairly jubilant at being able to help genuine Yankees."

Alonzo Jackson, a Georgetown, South Carolina, slave who ran a freight business, and his wife, a pastry chef, rescued ragged, starving, "weak . . . no shoes on" Yankees fleeing a Confederate prison at Florence. Though Mr. Jackson "wanted to be free—and wanted my race to be free," he and his wife first aided their white allies. Enemy patrols often threatened or fired at him, recalled Jackson, but "I fed and took them towards [the Union fleet at] North Island."

African-American women, Susie King wrote, also risked much for prisoners. "There were hundreds of them who assisted the

During the Civil War, slave runaways and Union soldiers united behind enemy lines.

Union soldiers by hiding them and helping them to escape. Many were punished for taking food to the prison stockades. . . . [In a Savannah stockade in 1865] soldiers were starving and these women did all they could towards relieving those men, although they knew the penalties should they be caught giving them aid. Others assisted in various ways the Union army. These things should be kept in history before the people."

Northerners expected that emancipation would trigger explosive rebellions that would disrupt the foe.

But southern slave patrols had been doubled, every adult white male was armed, and with Confederate units everywhere, rebellion became suicidal. President Lincoln emphasized that the Confederacy was "constituted on a basis entirely military. It would be easier now than formerly to repress a rising of unarmed and uneducated slaves."

The black *Christian Recorder* of Philadelphia answered those northerners who wanted a revolt: "Rise against what?—powder, cannon, ball, and grapeshot? Not a bit of it. They have got too much sense. Since you have waited till every man, boy, woman, and child in the so-called Southern Confederacy has been armed to the teeth, 'tis folly and mockery for you now to say to the poor, bleeding, and downtrodden sons of Africa, 'Arise and fight for your liberty!' "

By the summer of 1863, Confederate solidarity began to unravel under sustained attacks by black and white troops. The fall of Vicksburg and Port Hudson severed the Confederacy and brought the Yankees mastery of both sides of the Mississippi. To prevent the loss of their valuable property, slaveholders drove an estimated 150,000 slaves at gunpoint into Texas, a thousand miles from the advancing, liberating Yankees.

The invaders turned the South into churning confusion. Refugees clogged roads as black and white Union troops fanned out to overturn centuries of slaveholder domination. Outlaw bands that united Confederate and Union deserters with ex-slaves and Indians roamed the land foraging for food. Abandoned plantations were seized by the Union Army for recruiting stations for African-American men and as quarters for women and children.

A way of life began to collapse. Planters increasingly found their slaves fled, would not work, or insisted on pay. Slaves had begun to destroy the basis of white supremacy and slavery. The uncertainty of slave labor led to the steady dwindling of the Confederate food supply. As early as March 1863, a former Virginia governor wrote to the Confederate secretary of state about the impact of massive slave desertions. His melancholy report included: "Very little grain was raised last year, and less will be raised this year." He was worried about people "getting something to eat." By withholding their labor power, slaves were driving Confederate armies toward hunger and defeat.

In the turmoil of the southland, African-American fathers, mothers, and children tried to locate one another. They searched crowded "contraband" camps that began to dot the countryside. Some men and women set off to find their loved ones.

In 1863, in the border states, masters saw their slave system disintegrate before their eyes. Slaves seemed to melt away in Delaware, Missouri, and parts of Maryland. Since they were not touched by the Emancipation Proclamation, 44,300 chose enlistment in the Union Army as the route to freedom.

But their owners had other ideas and launched a new kind of warfare to stop enlistments. Masters formed armed posses that stationed themselves between their former slaves and their goal, the recruiters. Many an eager slave never reached the Union recruiting offices. Thousands were beaten, arrested, or slain. But still large numbers of African Americans in the border states ran to enlist.

The fall of Atlanta in September 1864 opened the road to freedom for hundreds of thousands in the Deep South. By December, General William Sherman, who vowed he would "have nothing to do with" the African-American population, began a sweep through Georgia to Savannah and the sea. A wave of black men, women, and children—equal in numbers to Sherman's army—picked up and followed in his wake.

One elderly slave told him, Sherman reported, he had been looking for "the 'Angel of the Lord' ever since he was knee-high, and though we professed to be fighting for the Union, he supposed that slavery was the cause, and that our success was to be his freedom." Did generals now listen to slaves talking politics?

Sherman changed his mind and relied on the full-scale use of armed African Americans to move his supplies to the front and protect his rear from Confederate raiders. A few days later General Grant also decided to make use of the masses of people who trailed after his invading army.

In January 1865, Sherman met with Savannah's African-American leaders. He issued Order #15, which handed abandoned

Slaves follow in the wake of General Sherman's march through the South.

coastland plantations from Charleston through the Georgia Sea Islands to former slaves who were willing to cultivate them. Hardly pausing after this radical land redistribution, Sherman wheeled his army into South Carolina, burning a dozen towns and shredding the state's slave system in the process.

Turmoil spread along country paths and city streets. Slaves spilled onto roads searching for relatives and sometimes clashed with Confederate soldiers trying to get home. Other slaves remained at home on abandoned plantations trying to bring in crops. Masters used guns to gather slaves for transportation to the interior, to Texas, to anywhere far from liberating armies.

By this time Sherman's foragers were raiding plantations in their path, and sometimes slave quarters as well. Food was taken from people who did not have enough to eat. Women who had been raped under slavery were now abused by northerners.

The line between slave and free African American in the South vanished as Confederates drafted free black men between eigh-

teen and fifty. Free and slave brother and sister, sometimes together, tried to flee their forced impressment for the safety of
Union or "contraband" camps.

Contraband camps became sanctuaries for thousands—dis-
placed persons trying to collect their families, calculate their next
move, and guess which direction pointed to safety. In the heart
of the Confederacy these camps became homes, educational networks, and experiments in African-American self-government.
Former slaves from Georgia and the Carolinas were taught how
to read and write by Union soldiers from Vermont and Minnesota. Former slaves from Alabama and Georgia told young
Yankee soldiers from Michigan and Kansas about what their
families had suffered. Everyone talked of a better future.

Southern whites complained about the "uppityness" or "in-
subordination" of slaves who slowed or left work, challenged
white rule, or simply slipped away. In South Carolina, twenty-
two irate slaveholders in March 1864 wrote the Confederate secretary of war saying their slaves were breaking into homes, hen and
meat houses, killing cattle and hogs, "and stealing everything
they can lay their hands on knowing we are not able to help
ourselves."

White resentment appeared in many forms. In Athens,
Georgia, free blacks danced around a liberty pole in the center of
town. At night whites cut it down. In Charleston, black troops
spent four days putting out fires, rescuing white people, and
guarding their property. But some Charlestonians, unwilling to
accept the new relations required by freedom, continued to insult
them. Slaves who escaped to enlist heard tales about their wives
and children being denied food or being beaten by revengeful
masters.

A constant stream of fugitives crossed into Union lines. In the
winter of 1864–65, T. Morris Chester, a young black reporter for
the *Philadelphia Press*, wrote: "The underground railroad, from

Richmond, seems to be thoroughly repaired and is not only in running condition, but is doing an increasing business. . . . For some time past we have had an arrival from Richmond every day, and not infrequently two or three times in the 24 hours. . . . Men, women, and children, of all colors, with their household effects, are daily coming into our lines."

Some escapees represented changing racial relations. A body servant risked his life to carry his wounded master to safety—then mounted his master's horse and rode off to the Yankees. One mistress told of an affectionate servant who nursed her through an illness and then suddenly "left me in the night." Another, whose denunciations of Yankees were published in Richmond papers, fled to Union lines bringing valuable information and twenty new Confederate uniforms.

When her servants suddenly disappeared, one mistress asked, "If they're not my slaves anymore, then whose are they?"

From Slave Liberation ...To Protest

THIRTEEN

The spirits of Gabriel Prosser, Denmark Vesey, Nat Turner, and hundreds of unknown rebels mingled with those in the ranks of the U.S. African-American armies of liberation. On a plantation near Richmond, Prosser had told his forces, "We have as much right to fight for our liberty as any men." Now slaves in U.S. uniforms rescued their Virginia sisters and brothers.

In Charleston, Vesey had told his followers, "We are fully able to conquer the whites if we were only unanimous and courageous." Now the sons and grandsons of his followers carried their regimental banners into Charleston and freed thousands. A vision of "white spirits and black spirits engaged in battle" told Turner to overturn bondage in Virginia. Now that sight was replayed each day in the Confederate states.

Armies of former slaves kept David Walker's promise—"Remember, Americans, that we must and shall be free." African-American bluecoats marched to the cadences of the Reverend Mr. Garnet's "Rather die freemen, than live to be slaves. . . . Let your motto be Resistance! Resistance! Resistance!"

With fixed bayonets and iron determination, African-American forces overran and captured their foes, and proved wrong a racial mythology that had held them in slavery. One column led off white prisoners singing, "O Massa a rebel, we row him to prison, Massa no whip us anymore." A soldier recognized his former owner among a group of prisoners and said, "Hi, massa— bottom rail on top this time!"

Black Union soldiers guarded Confederate prisoners. "The bottom rail is on top," said a former slave.

There were peaceful confrontations in which the newly freed slaves tried to explain a revolution had taken place. A former mistress asked her former slave, nineteen, "Why are you fighting against me?" He answered, "I ain't fighting you, I'm fighting to get free."

Slavery melted away with the appearance of black troops. They rescued families, protected women and children, emboldened runaways, and acted as an armed ally in the countryside for guerrilla units, families, and fugitives. As Frederick Douglass had predicted early in the war, the meaning of former slaves in U.S. Army uniforms would be a lesson not lost on friend or foe.

Harriet Tubman, now known as "General" Tubman, was invited to Hilton Head, South Carolina, to assist U.S. military operations. General Hunter asked her to accompany a Yankee raid on plantations along South Carolina's Combahee River.

On June 2, 1863, she led Colonel Montgomery's troops as they destroyed enemy railroad bridges and tracks. Tubman gathered up eight hundred rejoicing slaves. Later she described a wild scene along the riverbank as women swooped up their children, baskets, pigs, and chickens and jumped aboard federal gunboats. "All loaded. Pigs squealin'; chickens screamin'; young ones squallin'!" she recalled. "I never seen such a sight. We laughed and laughed and laughed."

African-American liberators touched the liberated with their electricity. A black U.S. sergeant said, "The change seems almost miraculous. The very people who, three years ago, crouched at their masters' feet, on the accursed soil of Virginia, now march in a victorious column of freedmen, over the same land." Another African-American soldier reported how they "stroll fearlessly and boldly through the streets."

There were unforgettable moments. "Men and women, old and young, were running through the streets, shouting and praising God," said a private in Wilmington, North Carolina. "We could truly see what we had been fighting for." A black sergeant added, "I could do nothing but cry to look at the poor creatures so overjoyed."

In Richmond, freed men and women asked Chaplain Garland White, accompanying the liberators, to give a speech about emancipation. Instead he broke into tears of "fullness of joy in my own heart." A few hours later the Reverend Mr. White was again overwhelmed when he was brought face-to-face with his enslaved mother, whom he had not seen in twenty years.

Infantrymen marched into events that lived with them forever. As bluecoats neared Richmond's Lumpkin's Jail, they heard fellow African Americans singing: "Slavery chain done broke at last! Gonna praise God till I die!"

A black soldier in Richmond described his regiment's effort: "We have been instrumental in liberating some five hundred of our sisters and brethren from the accursed yoke of human bondage."

The liberation moved Charles Fox, a white colonel who led the 55th Massachusetts Regiment into Charleston on February 18, 1865: "The few white inhabitants left in the town were either alarmed or indignant, and generally remained in their houses; but the colored people turned out en masse. . . . Cheers, blessings, prayers, and songs were heard on every side. Men and women crowded to shake hands with men and officers . . . the chorus of manly voices singing 'John Brown,' 'Babylon Is Falling,' and the 'Battle Cry of Freedom. . . .' The glory and triumph of this hour may be imagined, but can never be described. It was one of those occasions which happen but once in a lifetime, to be lived over in memory forever."

Emancipation repeatedly brought the joy of family reunions. In May 1865, a white Union officer wrote his wife: "Men are taking their wives and children; families which had been for a long time broken up are united and oh! such happiness. I am glad I'm here."

*   *   *

The 55th Massachusetts Regiment of ex-slaves and free blacks liberates Charleston, South Carolina, February 18, 1865.

Liberated slaves who served in the U.S. Army had their first taste of citizenship, demanding equal pay. What had been resistance to bondage shifted to the American right of protest. Trouble began when the Massachusetts and South Carolina enlistees, promised the $13 monthly pay of whites (plus a $3.50 clothing allowance), were paid $10 with $3 deducted for clothing.

Letters, petitions, and demonstrations by the 54th and 55th Massachusetts regiments demanded the promise be kept. Corporal James Henry Gooding, 54th Regiment, wrote to President Lincoln: "Not that our hearts ever flagged in Devotion, spite the evident apathy displayed on our behalf, but We feel as though our Country spurned us, now we are sworn to serve her." He asked: "We have done a soldier's Duty. Why can't we have a Soldier's pay?"

After discussing the pay issue with Frederick Douglass, Lincoln announced "ultimately they would receive the same." But impatient protesters boycotted payday. A 54th Regiment soldier wrote: "We quietly refused and continued our duty. For four months we have been steadily working day and night under fire."

Governor John A. Andrews called the Massachusetts legislature into special session, and it voted funds to make the pay equal. The troops rejected this offer on principle, a 55th Regiment soldier explaining, "We did not come to fight for money . . . we came not only to make men of ourselves, but of our colored brothers at home."

When Congress failed to equalize the pay, protests became more bitter. By late 1864, there was a near-mutiny in the 55th Regiment that lead to a court-martial and execution. Officers of the 54th were forced to shoot and wound two soldiers who refused to obey orders, and more than twenty black soldiers in the 14th Rhode Island Artillery were jailed.

Among the South Carolina troops, Sergeant William Walker led his volunteer company to the captain's tent. When they stacked their rifles and resigned, Walker was court-martialed and executed by firing squad. After eighteen months, Congress agreed to equalize pay retroactively. Sergeant James Ruffin of the 55th reported the victory: "We had a glorious celebration, there was a procession, then a mass meeting."

Former slaves in uniform eagerly sought liberty's other benefits. Between battles or huddled over flickering campfires at night, soldiers struggled to learn the alphabet. Many carried their spelling books with them to guard duty. A black sergeant wrote from

Union soldiers, books in hand, and their teachers represented an educational revolution.

Former slaves line up outside their Arlington, Virginia, school.

Virginia in March 1865: "A large portion of the regiment have been going to school during the winter months."

In Texas, Chaplain Thomas Stevenson wrote of his Kentucky regiment: "There is an ardent and universal desire among these men for books, especially those of an elementary character. . . . Nearly all of the men of my Regiment can spell and read with more or less accuracy, many can write with considerable mechanical excellence."

Sergeant John Sweeny, in Tennessee, wrote about "the necessity of having a school for the benefit of our regement [*sic*]. We have never Had an institution of that sort and we Stand deeply in need of the instruction, the majority of us having been slaves. We Wish to have some benefit of education To make ourselves capable of business In the future. We have estableshed [*sic*] a literary Association which flourished previous to our March to Nashville. We wish to become a People capable of self support as we are Capable of being soldiers."

Ex-slave Susie King, fourteen, began four years of service as a volunteer teacher: "I have about forty children to teach, besides a number of adults who come to me nights, all of them so eager to learn to read and write . . . above everything else."

The army experience taught more than reading and writing. The army chain of command became a vehicle for many former slaves seeking a redress of grievances. They petitioned their officers or sent letters to the War Department about slaveholder abuse of their families after husbands and fathers enlisted in the Union Army. Soldiers visiting wives still in bondage learned families had been punished because their men had enlisted.

Many requested aid in rescuing their wives and children. Captain Babcock, 12th U.S. Colored Artillery in Nashville, listened

Freedom meant an education. In Charleston, a slave-auction room is transformed into a classroom by African-American teachers and children.

to a black Tennessee soldier and then sent him and an armed squad of ten to rescue his wife. Private George Washington asked President Lincoln to release his wife and four children from slavery in Kentucky, one of the border states untouched by the Emancipation Proclamation. He wrote: "If you will free me and her and children with me, I can take Cair of them," and received no answer.

John Dennis asked the secretary of war for a pass to see his children, taken from him in 1859. As a slave father, he had only been allowed to visit them, and "it used to brake my heart" that "the man that they live with half feed them and half Cloth them & and beat them like dogs." Apologizing for "my Miserable writing," Dennis also asked, "I being Criple would like to know of you also if I Cant be permited to rase a School Down there."

Some letters complained to the president and the secretary of war of mistreatment of wives by white Union officers. "We are here and our wives and children are living out doers," wrote a Kentucky soldier. White officers, he said, called them "you damed bitches." The Kentuckian concluded: "It is now more than what a master would have done. . . . Shame, Shame, Shame how we are treated."

The right of peaceful protest often focused on the irritations of army life. "Instead of the musket it is the spade and the Wheelbarrow and the Axe cutting in one of the most horrible swamps in Louisiana stinking and miserable," wrote one soldier. Others expressed anger about "no chance to get home," "no pay," poor medical treatment, and new volunteers being beaten by white officers for failing to immediately grasp army routines.

Complaints alleged that white officers cheated their men or acted in old, bigoted ways. "We have been Treated more like Dogs than men," said one volunteer, and another claimed officers "beat the older soldiers." "There has not been one Indiana Colored Soldier who has deserted . . . and yet we are treated Like

Slaves," said one, pointing out, "We came to be true union soldiers, the Grandsons of Mother Africa Never to Flinch from Duty."

Soldiers used their new literary skills to write loved ones they were safe and would soon reunite their families. In 1864, Spottswood Rice wrote: "My Children . . . I have not forgot you and that I want to see you as bad as ever now my Dear Children I want you to be contented . . . be assured that I will have you if it cost me my life. Dont be uneasy my children . . . I expect to have you. . . . Oh! My Dear children how I do want to see you."

Soldiers received emotional letters from their wives. Alsie Thomas on a Louisiana plantation wrote four letters to her husband. "My children are going to school, but I find it hard to feed them all. . . . Come home as soon as you can, and cherish me as ever."

The war inspired African Americans in the North to demand that high officials insure just treatment for relatives in the U.S. Army. In 1863, Hannah Johnson, a Buffalo, New York, mother of a volunteer in the 54th Massachusetts Regiment, wrote President Lincoln demanding he intervene to halt the Confederate mistreatment of black prisoners. She proudly pointed out her father escaped from slavery in Louisiana, lamented her lack of a formal education, "but I know just as well as any what is right."

Of slaveholders, Mrs. Johnson said, "They have lived in idleness all their lives on stolen labor and made savages of the colored people, but they now are so furious because they [African-American troops] are proving themselves to be men." She concluded by asking the president to threaten retaliation against the Confederacy, "quickly and manfully, and stop this mean, cowardly cruelty. We your poor oppressed ones, appeal to you, and ask for fair play."

It was clear to former slaves who fought for freedom that their courage on the field of battle had paved the way for citizenship rights. Private Thomas Long was a former slave who served in the First South Carolina Volunteers. Asked to deliver the daily sermon one day to his fellow soldiers, Long reminded his fellow infantrymen of a painful legacy.

When they first enlisted, he said, "it was hardly safe" to pass white camps unless "we went in a mob and carried sidearms. But we whipped all dat down—not by going into the white camps for to whip em . . . but we lived it down by our natural manhood." He continued:

If we hadn't become soldiers, all might have gone back as it was before; our freedom might have slipped through de two houses of Congress and President Lincoln's years might have passed by and nothing been done for us. But now things can never go back, because we have showed our energy and our courage and our natural manhood.

Another thing is, suppose you had kept your freedom without enlisting in dis army; your children might have grown up free and been well cultivated so as to be equal to any business, but it would always have been flung in dere faces—'Your father never fought for he own freedom'—and what could dey answer? They never can say that to dis African Race anymore.

"At last came freedom. And what a joy it brought!" wrote Jacob Stroyer about his liberation in the spring of 1865. "The stars and stripes float in the air. The sun is just making its appearance from behind the hills, and throwing its beautiful light upon green bush and tree. The mocking birds and jay birds sing this morning more sweetly than before." Stroyer went on to become a successful minister in Salem, Massachusetts, where he wrote an autobiography.

Freedom did not bring equality, justice, or even happiness for all. A united country preserved much of its ancient prejudice and

Above: Freedom under assault. The KKK and other white supremacist groups began systematic attacks on the new black-white southern governments.

Below: The right to vote, granted former slaves in 1867, was meant to ensure all other rights.

introduced forms of bigotry better adapted to a new time. Those who had charged forward with poised rifle and bayonet to liberate their people had to face new enemies wielding not guns but pens. There were scholars, such as historian W. E. Woodward, who argued that African Americans "were the only people in the history of the world who became free without any effort of their own."

Bibliography

Aptheker, Herbert. *Abolitionism: A Revolutionary Movement.* Boston: Twayne Publishers, 1989.

———. *American Negro Slave Revolts.* New York: International Publishers, 1983 reprint.

———. *To Be Free.* New York: International Publishers, 1948.

———, ed. *A Documentary History of the Negro People in the United States,* vol. 1. New York: Citadel, 1951.

Banfield, Dr. Beryle. *The Resistance to Slavery.* N.Y.U. Race Desegregation Center: New York, 1988.

Berlin, Ira, et al., eds. *The Black Military Experience.* New York: Cambridge University Press, 1982.

———. *The Destruction of Slavery.* New York: Cambridge University Press, 1985.

Berry, Mary Francis. *Black Resistance/White Law.* Englewood Cliffs, N.J.: Prentice-Hall, 1971.

Blassingame, John W. *The Slave Community: Plantation Life in the Antebellum South.* New York: Oxford University Press, 1973.

———, ed. *Slave Testimonies.* Baton Rouge: Louisiana State University Press, 1978.

Bradford, Sarah. *Harriet Tubman: The Moses of Her People.* New York: Corinth Books, 1961 (reprint of 1886 edition).

Campbell, Stanley W. *The Slave Catchers*. New York: W.W. Norton, 1972.

Davidson, Basil. *The African Slave Trade*. Boston: Atlantic, Little Brown, 1961.

Doonan, Elizabeth. *Documents Illustrative of the History of the Slave Trade to America*, 4 vols. New York: Octagon Books, 1965 reprint.

Douglass, Frederick. *My Bondage and My Freedom*. New York: Arno Press, 1969 reprint.

Du Bois, W. E. B. *Black Reconstruction in America*. New York: World Publishing Company, 1962 reprint.

Franklin, John Hope. *From Slavery to Freedom*. New York: Knopf, 1985.

Genovese, Eugene D. *From Rebellion to Revolution*. New York: Vintage, 1981.

Giddings, Paula. *When and Where I Enter: The Impact of Black Women on Race and Sex in America*. New York: Bantam, 1985.

Gutman, Herbert G. *The Black Family in Slavery and Freedom 1750–1925*. New York: Pantheon, 1976.

Harding, Vincent. *There Is a River*. New York: Harcourt Brace Jovanovich, 1981.

Higginson, Thomas Wentworth. *Army Life in a Black Regiment*. New York: Collier Books, 1962 reprint.

———. *Black Rebellion*. New York: Arno Press, 1969 (Reprint of essays on Prosser, Vesey, and Turner slave rebellions).

Kaplan, Sidney. *The Black Presence in the Era of the American Revolution*. New York: Smithsonian Institution, 1973.

Katz, William Loren. *Black Indians: A Hidden Heritage*. New York: Atheneum, 1986.

———. *Eyewitness: The Negro in American History*. New York: Pitman, 1974.

———, ed. *Five Slave Narratives* (William Wells Brown, Moses Grandy, James W. C. Pennington, Lunsford Lane, Jacob Stroyer). New York: Arno Press, 1969.

Lauber, Almon W. *Indian Slavery in Colonial Times*. New York: Columbia University, 1913.

Lerner, Gerda, ed. *Black Women in White America*. New York: Vintage, 1983.

Logan, Rayford W., and Michael R. Winston, eds. *Dictionary of American Negro Biography*. New York: W.W. Norton, 1982.

McPherson, James L. *The Negro's Civil War*. New York: Pantheon, 1965.

Okihiro, Gary Y., ed. *In Resistance*. Amherst: University of Massachusetts Press, 1986.

Porter, Kenneth Wiggins. *The Negro on the American Frontier*. New York: Arno Press, 1971.

Price, Richard, ed. *Maroon Societies: Rebel Slave Communities in the Americas*. New York: Anchor Books, 1973.

Quarles, Benjamin. *Black Abolitionists*. New York: Oxford University Press, 1969.

————. *The Negro in the American Revolution*. Chapel Hill: University of North Carolina Press, 1961.

Rawick, George P., ed. *The American Slave: A Composite Autobiography*, 31 vols. Westport, Conn.: Greenwood Press, 1972, 1978.

Rose, Willie Lee. *Rehearsal for Reconstruction*. New York: Vintage, 1967.

Stampp, Kenneth M. *The Peculiar Institution*. New York: Vintage, 1956.

Starobin, Joseph. *Industrial Slavery in the Old South*. New York: Oxford University Press, 1970.

Sterling, Dorothy, ed. *We Are Your Sisters: Black Women in the Nineteenth Century*. New York: W.W. Norton, 1984.

Still, William. *The Underground Railroad*. New York: Arno Press, 1969.

Williams, Eric. *From Columbus to Castro: The History of the Caribbean*. New York: Vintage, 1984 reprint.

Wood, Peter H. *Black Majority*. New York: Knopf, 1974.

Woodson, Carter G. *The Education of the Negro Prior to 1861*. New York: Arno Press, 1969 reprint.

W.P.A. Study. *The Negro in Virginia*. New York: Arno Press, 1969 reprint.

Index